I0772910

iii

Mary Pickford Mystery

By William Baer

For my family and friends

"America's Sweetheart"

1. El Matador

Tuesday, February 4, 1919

"Do you have a gun?"

It was the soft voice of the most famous woman in the world.

She was concerned.

Yet calm.

"Yes," I said.

"Bring it."

I'd been sitting on the back deck of the small guest house behind Mary's hideaway cottage on the Malibu bluffs above El Matador. It was late at night, but the moon was strong and silver over the Pacific. Beneath the cliffs, I could see the dark sandy beach and the outlines of some of the peculiar sea stacks and rock formations. Then the phone rang, and it was my boss. Gladys Smith. Better known as Mary Pickford, whom over fifteen million Americans spend their money to see at their local movie theater every single day.

Which doesn't even count the filmgoers in all the other countries in the world.

Mary explained.

"There's a man staggering around the garden, and I think he has a gun. He's calling out my name."

"I'm on my way, Miss Mary!"

I grabbed my Colt New Service Revolver and headed toward the garden.

Yeah, I was just her temporary chauffeur, but I'd grown up on my old man's cattle ranch near Tucson, Arizona, and I knew how to handle a gun.

Despite the high moon, the garden was midnight dark. I could see Miss Mary standing outside, just as she might have looked in one of her movies. Tiny, lovely, innocent, and entirely unafraid.

I didn't like it.

"You need to get back in the cottage," I said, a bit more firmly than I'd ever spoken to her before.

She didn't mind.

"I'm fine, Billy," she said softly, "you'll protect me if it's needed."

Which seemed like a lot of responsibility for an eighteen-year-old former ranch hand.

Then I saw him coming toward us in the darkness.

He seemed to be disorientated.

He seemed to be staggering a bit, holding a revolver in his right hand, so I lifted mine and pointed it at his chest.

"Stop right there!" I said.

He did, but his balance was uncertain.

Then he saw Mary standing behind me.

"Miss Pickford?" he called out weakly.

But then he collapsed to the ground in a heap.

Before I could make a move, Mary was rushing over to the man and kneeling above him, trying to help.

When I stepped closer, she looked up at me.

"He's been shot, Billy. At least once."

"With a Springfield '80," the man said, rather deliriously.

"What's that?" Mary asked me confusedly.

"It's a trapdoor breech-loading rifle," I explained. "Very rare and not very reliable."

Mary took the man's head into her arms.

He seemed to be about forty or so, nicely dressed, rather ordinary looking, and quickly losing consciousness.

"I know this man," Mary said.

He looked up into her eyes.

"Help her," he said weakly.

Then his head sank back, and he shut his eyes, and everything else shut down as well.

"Is he dead?" Mary asked.

"Yes."

Gently, she lay his head back on the ground, then stood up, thinking things over.

"Who is he?" I asked.

"His name is Burke. I met his wife recently. She's a young actress, and I tried to help her out. Her name is Bonnie Burke."

"So I'm guessing that she's the one he wants you to help?" I suggested.

Mary nodded and took charge.

"You stay right here, Billy. I'll go inside and call Kaplan."

Howard Kaplan was Adolph Zukor's lawyer. He was a man who could "fix" anything.

"What about the cops?" I asked.

"He'll take care of it."

Which is exactly what happened.

Kaplan and three cops arrived soon afterward. Eventually, an ambulance came and took care of the dead body.

Mary and I explained what had happened to the cops, except for the "Help her" bit, and that was that.

Not really.

After they were gone, Mary stood in the moonlight and looked up at me. I'm 6'1", and she's a flat five feet.

"We won't say anything about this, Billy."

I knew exactly *what* she meant and *whom* she meant.

Her mom and Douglas.

(Douglas Fairbanks.)

"There's no need to concern anyone else," she explained.

"Of course," I agreed.

Then she looked into my eyes, conspiratorially.

"We'll figure this out on our own."

Which meant that Mary Pickford wasn't going to let some man with a gun die in her garden without getting to the bottom of it.

Which was fine with me.

2. United Artists

Wednesday, February 5, 1919

The lunatics have taken over the asylum.

Or is it "the inmates"?

I can't remember.

The day after Burke died in her garden, Mary Pickford, as if nothing unusual had happened the previous night, met with DW Griffith, Charles Chaplin, and Douglas Fairbanks and created United Artists.

Shaking up the entire film industry.

Even I, who knew very little about the inner workings of Hollywood, knew that it was an audacious move. Extremely risky. Could three movie stars and the world's most famous director really set up their own distribution company and make it work? Mary had no doubt about it, and she was the driving force behind the incorporation. Yes, it was true that she was universally known as "America's Sweetheart," but she was also a very astute businesswoman.

A poverty-stricken youth can do that to you sometimes.

Regardless, along with her mother Charlotte and a phalanx of corporate lawyers, they all signed the agreement. They would each independently produce four films every year for the next three years and release them exclusively though United Artists.

It was essentially a rebellion against her former boss Adolph Zukor who was planning to combine his own company, Famous Players-Paramount, with his main rival, First National Pictures, in an attempt to take control of Hollywood distribution. If Zukor and First National succeeded, they'd be able to contain and control the actors' rising salaries, like those of Mary and Chaplin who were making over a million a year. They could also manipulate the market with block booking. Which meant, for example, promising a theater the next Pickford film only if it agreed to purchase a bunch of other less-marketable films.

Unfortunately for Zukor, when the UA rebels got wind of the scheme, they hired a female Pinkerton agent to infiltrate Zukor's private meetings at the Alexandria Hotel where she was able to verify the forthcoming merger.

Ironically, Mary had made many of her most famous pictures with Adolph Zukor: *The Poor Little Rich Girl*, *Rebecca of Sunnybrook Farm*, *A Little Princess*, etc.

Also ironically, just six months ago, Mary had left Zukor for First National when her contract renewal broke down, and she still owed First National several pictures.

Even more ironically, Mary and Zukor, despite their famous contract disputes, were still very close. I suspect that, in a way, Zukor was like the father that Mary had never known. She and Zukor remained the best of pals, and she still called him "Papa Zukor," and he still called her "Sweetheart-honey."

Which seemed a little weird to me.

But, hell, it's a weird world in general, and I was learning very quickly that Hollywood was far weirder than all the rest of the weird world.

So what was the likes of me doing there anyway?

A few months ago, Mary's regular driver got sick, and her friend Will S. Hart recommended me. So I did my best, and I ended up doing a lot more than just driving when Mary came down with Influenza early last month. I soon became her "please do this, Billy" and "please do that, Billy" helper-boy while she recuperated. Fortunately, I'd already had the Spanish Flu myself, and it didn't hit Mary as hard as her close friend Lilian Gish who'd nearly died of the flu last August and was out of action for over four months. So I became indispensable, and it was much appreciated by Mary and her mother Charlotte.

Now that the UA contracts were signed, Mary was supposed to "take it easy" and rest for a couple of weeks before resuming her rigorous schedule and her next picture. Which is why she was staying out in Malibu at the Matador cottage, twenty-five miles from downtown Los Angeles.

That evening, I drove her back to the beach.

"How did it go, Miss Mary?" I asked.

"Fine, Billy, but tomorrow we've got other stuff to do."

"I'm ready to go."

Of course, I had no idea *exactly* what she meant, but I was ready to do anything for Miss Mary Pickford.

"We've got a week or so," she explained, "before my mom gets back."

"I'm ready to go," I repeated.

I knew that her mom was leaving town tomorrow to visit relatives in Toronto.

I also knew that the other main distraction in Mary's life was also leaving town for a shoot somewhere in Nevada.

Her lover and now her business partner.

Douglas Fairbanks.

3. Forest Lawn

Thursday, February 6, 1919

Well, it sure doesn't look like a graveyard!

According to the pamphlet, the guy who built the place found graveyards "ugly and depressing," so he decided to build one that was cultivated like a garden with cheerful flowers, comforting fountains, happy birds, and majestic trees.

But in the end, let's face it, even here at lovely Forest Lawn in Glendale, you're still dropping a dead body into a hole in the ground. Which they were currently doing with the mortal remains of Philip Burke who'd died at my feet two nights ago in the arms of Mary Pickford.

I was standing off by the car beneath a stand of oaks and watching from a distance. It was sparsely attended. Maybe eight people not counting the priest and the cemetery staff. Burke's young widow was clearly distraught and struggling. Some young guy in a grey suit stood nearby solicitously, but he seemed afraid to touch her. A few more mourners stood around the open grave in silence.

Apparently, the Burkes had come to LA from San

Francisco a few months ago hoping to get some acting work for Bonnie. Mary had run into her at Biograph, and she took a liking to the young girl and even got her a bit part on DW Griffith's current production. The Burkes, of course, were extremely grateful, and Mary apparently said something like, "If I can be of any help, just let me know." Which is why Philip Burke, with two rifle shots in his back, showed up in Malibu two nights ago.

"How did he know about El Matador?" I'd asked Mary earlier.

She shrugged.

"The Malibu hideaway was mentioned in a recent *Photoplay* article. Maybe that's what gave him the idea to try Malibu when he couldn't find me in LA."

Maybe.

As for Mary, she was standing within the small crowd of mourners. Everyone knew who she was, of course, but they did their best not to stare, given the circumstances. I did wonder why Bonnie Burke had decided to bury her husband in Glendale rather than take the body back to San Francisco where surely more people would have shown up for his burial.

I also wondered why the burial had happened so quickly.

Oh, well, who knows?

When the priest was done and the handfuls of dirt were tossed, Mary stepped over and consoled the devastated young wife, who held onto Mary like a lifelong friend. Eventually, when she let her go, Mary commiserated for a while, but I was too far away to hear the conversation.

[Billy, I think you need to tell your readers who you are. You were much more than just my driver. Give your own background. Your readers will want to know.]

I've been advised to write a little bit about myself, so here goes. If it's too dull or seemingly irrelevant, please skip ahead:

I was born on my family's cattle ranch west of Tucson eighteen years ago. My mom, Marita Rosalita Kidd, was a Mexican seamstress with a strain of Apache, and my old man, Captain William Thomas Kidd, was a third-generation Arizonan from mostly Scot roots. Aside from overseeing the family cattle ranch (roughly 800 head), he also served as an Arizona Ranger (1901-1909) and the reluctant sheriff of Tucson (1915-1917), which he did from a sense of duty.

I was the Kidd's second and last child, being twelve years younger than my older, now-married brother Thomas. I grew up perfectly content on Big K Ranch, loving horses, rodeo, novels (Dickens, Thackeray, etc.), and eventually the flickers. I was always called Billy, never Will or William or Willie, and I can never remember a time when I wasn't called "Billy the Kid" in reference to you-know-who.

Or sometimes just "the Kid."

I was raised right, never drink, pray sometimes, always try to be friendly, and never back down from a fight. I write my mom a letter every two weeks.

When I was eight years old, I saw my first flicker in a Tucson nickelodeon. It was DW Griffith's Biograph short *The Girl and the Outlaw*, in which there was a very pretty young extra named Florence Lawrence, who eventually became Griffith's first recognizable star before Mary came along and changed everything.

So I got hooked on the flicks.

The following year, I saw Tom Mix win several trophies at the Prescott Frontier Days Rodeo, and I got to meet him five years later when I entered my first rodeo at the age of fourteen. He was a hell of a rider and roper and shooter, and he encouraged me and helped me a lot. The next year, I won my first riding trophy at Prescott, somehow surviving on a monster bull from Texas named "Bloodshot."

The following year, my old man deputized me for a manhunt for the notorious Red Rock rustler and outlaw John Turner Drover whom we caught near the Mexican border at Sasabe. In the subsequent skirmish, Drover and his two companions ended up dead.

As you can see, I was leading a very exciting young life as a carefree young ranch hand and occasional rodeo rider. My brother Tom had married, and I knew that he'd take over the ranch someday, which left me free to do whatever I wanted to do.

"Don't be too frivolous," my old man would warn me, and I tried not to be.

Then the big trouble kicked up in Europe, and I volunteered for Blackjack Pershing's Expeditionary Force on my eighteenth birthday, which initiated quite a year! I was immediately sent for training at Camp Funston at Fort Riley near Manhattan, Kansas, just in time for the sudden appearance of the Influenza, which we took along with us to Europe, infecting most of the French troops, about half of the Brits, and over a million Huns, not to mention the millions of non-combatants who got caught up in the worldwide epidemic. The soon misnamed "Spanish Flu."

As for me, I saw some limited combat with General Winn's 89th Division during a few skirmishes near Mourmelon-le-Grand before the disease dropped me on my back and they sent me back to the States to recuperate. After a rather unpleasant month or so, having been discharged from the army, I hooked up with Tom Mix's summer rodeo tour which initiated at the 101 Ranch near Ponca City in northern Oklahoma, then migrated throughout the West.

In August, at a show near Los Angeles, I got tossed by a big ugly sucker named "Death's Head," and damaged my left shoulder. I ended up in a local army hospital where I had a most fortunate encounter with Will S. Hart. The most famous movie star of the Western flickers stopped by the hospital to cheer up the veterans, and he came over to my bed, learned that I was a "rider," and took an immediate interest.

Then he shocked me.

"How'd you like to drive me around town?" he asked.

It turned out that his regular driver was getting married the following week, and Mr. Hart had promised him a month's vacation.

"Sounds great, Mr. Hart!"

"Call me, Will."

"Yes, sir."

Four days later, I was driving one of the most famous men in the world around town in his Duesenberg Model A. I knew it was just temporary, but it was still quite marvelous. Four fascinating weeks of movie sets, famous actors, famous executives, famous writers, and famous Hollywood wranglers (all of whom were former ranch guys like myself, who were known as the "Gower Gulch Gang" and hung out at the Sunset Corral and worked as film extras, and who always called me "Billy the Kid").

But it couldn't last forever.

Then, amazingly, something even more amazing happened.

I met his dear friend Mary Pickford.

Whose driver (who will go unnamed) had seriously injured himself in a crash near San Bernardino (apparently drunk), so she needed a new driver.

I couldn't believe my good fortune.

Thank you, ugly Death's Head, for wrecking my shoulder!

So I started working for Mary three months ago and became not only her driver, but a jack-of-all trades and gofer for both Mary and her mom Charlotte who lived together in a little house at 56 Fremont Place in Los Angeles.

Immediately, I felt part of the team, if not the family, even before Mary got hit with Influenza last month. I moved her mom to the Beverly Hills Hotel and took care of Mary all by myself. She was very stoic about it all, and I did my best, and we became very close. I'd like to believe that she came to think of me as her little brother, even though she already had one.

These days I'm driving Miss Mary Pickford all around LA, watching her deal with all kinds of famous people. And some of the not-so-famous as well. Like Bonnie Burke, currently standing over the open grave of her dead husband.

I noticed that one of the mourners, a young woman, was now standing near me, also watching Mary doing her best to comfort Bonnie Burke. Like Mary, the young woman was wearing a dark dress with a dark hat and a dark veil. The veil was now pulled up. She had long blonde wavy hair and was attractive as hell. A girl-next-door knockout.

I walked over, and she looked right into my eyes with her drop-dead blue ones.

"You're Miss Pickford's driver, right?"

"Yes, Billy Kidd. And you?"

"I'm a friend of Bonnie's from San Francisco. Wendy Parker."

We shook hands, and we talked a bit. She'd worked with Bonnie at some film distribution firm in SF, and she wasn't at all surprised that Bonnie had come to LA.

"She's always wanted to be in films."

"Not you?" I smiled.

"Not really. But I suppose every girl thinks about it from time to time."

"Especially the pretty ones," I said, wondering if I was laying it on a bit too thick.

She smiled anyway.

I wanted to try and make her smile again, but I knew what I *should* be doing. Getting more information. After all, I was now the assistant to Detective Mary Pickford.

"What did her husband do?"

She shrugged.

"Clerical stuff. Office stuff. He got a job at one of the smaller studios in LA, but he was fired last week."

"Why?"

She hesitated at first, then decided to confide.

"I heard it was drink, but there were also rumors about narcotics."

I was surprised, astonished.

"Do you think it's possible?"

She shrugged again, which I very much enjoyed.

"Which studio?"

"Brunton."

Over near the grave, I could see Mary handing Bonnie the check she'd written earlier in the car. Mary had grown up poor, but now she was fabulously wealthy, and she was very generous. Very charitable. My salary is proof of that!

I got back to business.

"Who's that guy lurking around over there?" I said referring to the hovering guy in the gray suit.

"I don't know."

"He seems very interested in Bonnie."

"Yes, he certainly does."

She looked at me and smiled, and I wondered the only thing worth wondering.

Should I ask her for a date?

4. Brunton Studios

Thursday, February 6, 1919

I didn't like the guy.

I could tell that Mary felt the same way.

His name was Maurice Kauffman, and he ran Brunton Studios over on Melrose. When we arrived, Mary and I were immediately ushered into his office. After all, who in this town would keep Mary Pickford waiting?

He was a small thin balding guy in a dark suit, who did his cringing best to be solicitous to Mary, but I could tell that he was edgy.

Nervous.

Maybe that was good.

Earlier, Mary and her new UA business partners had done a reenactment of the contract signing for the press at Chaplin Studios, then posed for subsequent photos at Griffith Studios. Throughout it all, Mary was her usual charming playful self, but I knew that she had other things on her mind. Afterward, on the short drive to Brunton Studios, she made it clear that I was in "this thing" one hundred percent.

"I'll be introducing you as my consultant, Billy,"

she said.

Even though I liked that a lot, I still laughed.

"An eighteen-year-old consultant?"

Mary smiled.

"Yes, you'll need to act precocious."

"I'll do my best, but what if they see me driving the car?"

She shrugged.

"So what if they do?"

Exactly.

Who's going to question Mary Pickford in this town?

She shook hands with Maurice Kauffman.

"This is my consultant, William Kidd."

He smiled at me with complete disinterest, and we shook hands.

"How can I help you, Miss Pickford?"

Mary was never one to waste time.

"I want to know why you fired Philip Burke?"

Immediately, the little creep got spooked.

"We felt that his work was unsatisfactory," he explained evasively.

"In what way?"

Kauffman tried to conjure something that might make some sense.

"Well, he was often late. Not punctual at all. And we found errors in his calculations."

"What calculations?"

"He worked in the finance department."

Mary stared at him.

I'd seen her do it before. Thankfully, never at me. Yes, Mary was America's Sweetheart, but she also had absolutely no tolerance for ineptitude, malingering, or prevarication.

She stared at the prevaricator in silence. It seemed like an hour, and even I got a bit nervous. Finally, she spoke.

"Are you finished lying, Mr. Kauffman?"

Kauffman made no effort to deny it. I think he was just glad the silent "Mary stare" was over.

Mary continued.

"Do you think people in this industry would like to know that you've been lying about one of your employees who was murdered two nights ago?"

"No," he admitted.

It was the tiniest wimpiest "no" I'd ever heard.

"So what's this nonsense about alcohol?"

"It's untrue," he admitted.

"Narcotics?"

"Also untrue."

"Did he have any enemies here?"

"No."

"Then why did you fire him?"

The tiny man behind his huge desk pointed upward. Gingerly.

"It came from above."

Which seemed to be what Mary had assumed.

"From whom?"

I could actually see the sweat streaking on the guy's forehead.

"If I say that, Miss Pickford, I'll be fired as well."

Mary believed him, so she kept it general.

"From the top?"

"Yes."

"Zukor?"

"Yes, from the top. That's the best I can do."

Naturally, I was knocked for a loop, but I didn't let on.

Did Zukor have a hand in this?

In what way?

When Mary stood up, I did the same and held the door. Then she turned around and looked at Kauffman one last time.

"Did you ever meet Mr. Burke's wife?"

"No."

I believed him.

So did Mary.

Then we were gone.

5. Topanga Canyon

Thursday, February 6, 1919

I pulled the Packard Twin Six in front of the Burke's little yellow cottage in Topanga Canyon.

Mary wanted to check on the grieving widow.

She also had a long list of questions that she didn't feel were appropriate this morning at the cemetery.

We walked up to the front door, and she knocked.

Nothing.

Maybe Mrs. Burke wasn't home.

Mary, persistent as always, knocked again.

Then we heard something.

"Is that what it sounds like?" I said stupidly.

It was a crying child.

I looked at Mary.

"I didn't know she had a child," I said.

"She doesn't."

Mary took hold of the doorknob, and the door was unlocked. When she stepped inside the cottage, I followed.

The place had clearly been tossed.

I pulled out my Colt.

"Bonnie?" Mary called out softly. "It's Mary

Pickford."

The only response was more crying, which we followed into a small bedroom. A discontented baby boy was lying on the bed. I don't know much about kids, but this one was *very* young. Maybe a month or so.

Mary immediately picked up the child to comfort him.

Which worked.

"I'll check the rest of the place," I said. "You stay right here."

I checked all the rooms in the small cottage and found Bonnie lying on the floor in the other bedroom. She was still wearing black, and it was clear that she'd been strangled. She been strangled so hard, that there was blood leaking from the red bruise around her neck.

"Is she dead?" Mary asked from behind me, having ignored my instructions. She was still holding the baby, and she seemed as calm as Jane Eyre witnessing the horrors in Rochester's attic.

"Yes," I confirmed.

Mary nodded, went into the small living room, and dialed a number on the house phone.

I was certain that it was Kaplan again.

She was soon connected.

"Bonnie Burke is dead. Murdered. When you come, bring Grayson."

Gregory Grayson was the LA detective who'd come to Malibu two nights ago and was working the Philip Burke case. Now he could work the dead wife's case as well.

Mary gave Kaplan directions to the cottage.

"There's also a child here, a baby," she added, "so

call Mrs. Hilder at Maternal Charities."

Which was one of the local charities that Mary supported.

An hour later, after Eleanor Hilder had taken the child away, Grayson was still searching through the cottage, which I'd already done before he arrived. There wasn't much. The Burkes had very few possessions and very few business records. Just some recent receipts and a bank statement with $34.57 left in a checking account.

It was strange.

After talking with Grayson, I went out back where Mary was sitting on a little porch and staring up the sides of the canyon. Beneath her, there was a small athletic bag that was lying open on the floor.

"Some guy," I explained, "was lurking across the street in a city taxi."

Mary was interested, so I told her more.

"I told Grayson about it, but when we started walking over there, the cab took off."

"Did you get a look?"

"Not really, just some non-descript guy, maybe twenty-five or so."

When Mary nodded, I sat down beside her.

She seemed to have a lot on her mind.

So did I.

"What do you make of the baby?" I tried.

Mary shrugged.

"I don't think it's Bonnie's."

"Somebody else's?" I suggested foolishly.

She didn't respond.

"Well," I said hopefully, "if it's an orphan, maybe somebody will adopt it."

Mary shrugged again, as she thought back into her distant past.

"I was nearly adopted, Billy," she said, "when we were down and out in Toronto."

Since I was naturally curious, she told me more about it.

Mary, who was known as "Gladys" back then, was about five years old at the time, and her mother was having great difficulties putting food on the table for her three young children. Then Dr. George B. Smith and his kindly wife took an interest in Mary and offered to adopt her. At first, Charlotte was horrified by the idea, but she also wanted the best for her oldest child. So one day they went to visit the wealthy Smiths, and Mary was naturally attracted by their lovely home, the promise of endless ice cream, and the promise of a pony and cart. Afterward, when Mary realized what it actually meant, she told her mother tearfully, "I don't want to be Dr. Smith's little girl. I want to go home with you, Mama!" So they cried together and that was the end of that.

"Is that why you support the local Orphans Asylum?"

"Yes."

6. Million Dollar Theatre

Thursday, February 6, 1919

It wasn't just a movie theater, it was a movie palace!

I'd read about it, of course, but it was much more amazing than I'd imagined. It was also amazing to think that my first film experience was in a tiny nickelodeon in Tucson ten years ago, and now I was walking into Sid Grauman's Million Dollar Theatre on Broadway with over two thousand seats inside.

Even the elaborate exterior, with its huge marquee and its architectural ornamentations (in something called Spanish Baroque Revival style), didn't prepare me for the interior, with a magnificent chandelier hanging from a coffered-dome ceiling. With a marvelous winged female high above the huge proscenium. With a massive balcony. With colorful murals representing Ruskin's popular fairy tale, *The King of the Golden River*. With the biggest organ (Wurlitzer) I'd ever seen.

Etc.

Grauman opened his palace fifteen months ago, featuring Will S. Hart's latest film, *The Silent Man*, which was attended by every big shot in Hollywood: all the politicians, Chaplin, Fairbanks, and, of course, Mary Pickford.

Tonight, I was here to see a preview of Mary's new picture with the ironic title *Captain Kidd, Jr.*, which I hope my old man (who was a *real* Captain Kidd) will eventually get to see in Tucson.

I wasn't alone tonight.

I had a pretty young woman on my arm.

Wendy Parker.

Whom I'd met this morning amid the dead and the graves at Forest Lawn Cemetery.

"Why don't we do something tonight?" I tried after we'd talked for awhile.

She smiled.

"I guess cowboys don't waste any time."

(She'd already asked me about my background.)

So I gave her an appropriate cowboy shrug.

She thought it over.

"What do you have in mind, Billy?"

"How about a movie? What else?"

She laughed.

I liked her laugh.

"Sure, why not?"

She was no longer dressed in cemetery black. She wore a light blue pleated skirt that stopped a few inches below her knees. With a matching sleeveless top. With white gloves and white T-strap shoes. With a small white bucket hat.

Very fashionable, even in such a fashionable environment. Even in a town flush with pretty young women, Wendy caught lots of eyes, both male and female, walking down the center aisle.

The film had been directed by William Desmond Taylor, and it was set to be officially released in early April. It was written by one of Mary's best friends, Frances Marion, and it was shot by one of her favorite cinematographers, Charles Rosher.

Given the title, as you might expect, it's about a treasure hunt.

Mary plays Mary MacTavish who lives with her grandfather who runs a second-hand bookstore, where she happily reads books by Kipling, Alcott, Stevenson, and the Brontës. As well as the plays of Shakespeare. Then one day, Mary finds a treasure map in one of the old books. It was placed there by a very wealthy man, now deceased, who mentioned it in his last will and testament. Eventually, Mary and her boyfriend Jim (Douglas MacLean) team up with the wealthy man's grandson (Willie Carleton) to search for the treasure. The map leads them to a farm where they do a lot of digging and finally find the treasure box which contains nothing but a note from the deceased man. The note explains that it was all a test to encourage his grandson to lead a healthy and active life. Everything, of course, ends happily, as Willie receives his trust, and Mary and Jim get engaged.

It was a wonderful film, and Wendy and the rest of the audience enjoyed it just as much as I did. Mary was her natural, charming, spirited self, playing the kind of young woman that had endeared her to audiences all over the world. I had no doubt that it would be a huge hit.

I also couldn't ignore the ironies.

Mary and I were currently underway on a mystery of our own. One with even more at stake. A dead man and a dead woman.

Afterward, Wendy and I remained in our seats and talked about the movie.

And about Mary.

"She's so natural, Billy! Always so believable!" she marveled.

It was true, and I'd learned a lot more about it from Mary's mom Charlotte. Even as a young girl on the stage, Mary believed in a more realistic style of acting, more in the mode of Eleonora Duse than the usual histrionics of most of the denizens of the American stage. She was further encouraged to perform that way by David Belasco, and when she went to work in films with Griffith, she again muted her performances in contrast to the highly gestured over-dramatic acting styles of the early films. It definitely gave her a more expressive range and more psychological depth, and audiences responded accordingly.

I explained some of this to Wendy, trying not to sound too much like a chauffeur know-it-all.

"And what's with her eyes, Billy?" Wendy asked. "Are they really like that?"

"Yes."

"What color?"

"Hazel."

It's definitely true that Mary had big round tender beautiful eyes. Apparently, Griffith once called them "sparkling Irish eyes" with "languorous capabilities."

Whatever that means.

"I'd love to meet her sometime," Wendy decided.

I smiled.

"Maybe you will."

Wendy smiled as well, then she thought of

something else.

"Why aren't you driving her tonight?"

"She's working at home on her next movie."

"What's it called?"

"*Daddy-Long-Legs*. Mary's writing it herself with some help from her friend Frances Marion."

"The woman who wrote tonight's film?"

"Exactly."

Somewhere in the midst of all this, I noticed that Wendy had placed her hand over mine.

I was more than pleased!

7. Daddy-Long-Legs

Friday, February 7, 1919

I was sitting in the very comfortable living room of the Malibu cottage with Mary and Frances Marion.

Feeling quite uncomfortable.

We were gathered together to discuss Mary's scenario for her next movie, *Daddy-Long-Legs*.

But what the hell was *I* doing here?

Good question.

It all started about a week ago when I was driving Mary back from a location scout in Santa Barbara. Mary was sitting in the back seat of the Packard silently working on something, and I was enjoying the pleasant drive south along the Pacific coast. Then she finished whatever she was doing, and she asked me a question that I certainly wasn't prepared for.

"What do you want to do with your life, Billy?"

She had a knack for asking important questions when they were least expected. I guess she didn't believe that I was planning to drive people around in their cars for the rest of my life.

Initially, I was evasive.

Quite evasive.

"When I was a young boy on my father's ranch, I thought mostly about winning rodeo trophies, even though I knew that a life like that could never last forever. Then the war came, and I wrecked my shoulder, and I ended up driving for Mr. Hart."

All of which she knew.

"So what do you want to do with the rest of your life?" she repeated.

Apparently, I wasn't going to get off that easy.

"Well, it might seem rather ridiculous," I warned her.

"Tell me."

Which I did.

"I'd like to write stories, Mary. I've been obsessed with stories ever since I was a kid."

I could see Mary in the rear-view mirror, and she didn't seem to think it was such a ridiculous notion, which made me feel comfortable talking about it.

(Note: you might be tempted to skip this chapter, which is fine with me, but it does explain how *this* particular murder story could eventually be written.)

[Good idea.]

"When did it start?"

"When I was a little kid. My grandfather, who was a desert Mexican with some Apache thrown in, told me all kinds of marvelous stories as I followed him around the ranch. My old man could also tell an impressive good story, and so could some of the old ranch hands at night in the bunkhouse. My old man had been a cattleman all of his life, except for some law enforcement stints in Tucson and with the Arizona

Rangers, but he was quite a reader, with a surprisingly sizable library. One day, he called me into his office, and he handed me a book and said, 'You like stories, William? Then read this one. Then read everything else in the library.'"

"What was it?"

"*Riders of the Purple Sage.*"

"Zane Grey?"

"Yes."

"Didn't Will Farnum just star in a version of that book last year?"

"Yes," I agreed, "and not a bad version. He played Lassiter. The gunfighter."

Mary nodded, then turned the conversation back to me.

"So you read it, right?"

"Right, and I loved it. Lots of twists and turns. With a kidnapping, rustling, gunfights, and some spooky Mormons."

"How old were you at the time?"

"Twelve. So I went back to my father, and I asked him for more, and he said, 'Fine, William, read all the Zane Greys you want, but read the other stuff too and start with the Brits.' Then he thought it over a moment and said, 'Maybe start with *The Virginians*.' So I did."

"What's that?"

"It's a peculiar novel by Thackeray, whom I'd never heard of before. It's about a young Englishman who served under General Wolfe at the capture of Quebec, but who later sided with the colonies during the Revolutionary War."

"Was it any good?"

"It was certainly interesting. It was way too long,

and it rambled too much, but it opened me up to the world of English literature. Soon I was reading the Brontës, Dickens, and Austen. Then Shakespeare. Then I tried other stuff like *One Thousand and One Nights*, Edgar Allan Poe, and O. Henry."

I tried to explain myself.

"It was essentially my education. My parents had a history tutor come to the ranch sometimes for me and my brother, but mostly we were off working with the cattle and working the stables."

"Did you try to write yourself?"

Mary, as always, could see right through me. She could see where all this was leading, and she got right to it. But it was always something that I'd kept to myself. It seemed rather preposterous that an Arizona ranch hand would want to be a published writer, so I'd only confided my thoughts to my mother, then later to my father.

Nevertheless, as I've already mentioned, Mary always made me feel comfortable about things that were uncomfortable.

"I did."

"What?"

"Some dreadful poems and a few absurd short stories."

"Tell me one."

Which naturally knocked me back a bit.

But I did my best to keep my eyes on the road, as I did what I was told to do. I told her about "Sundown," a story about a young Arizona rancher in 1884 who comes up with a dangerous plan to help his politician brother secure statehood for the Arizona Territory.

"I'm still working on that one," I said defensively.

"I like it. Tell me another. Something different."

So I told her the narrative line of "Shroud" which is about the murder of a famous scientist who's trying to debunk the authenticity of the Shroud of Turin.

That one certainly seemed "different" enough.

"I like it, Billy. Give me one more."

So I synopsized "The Plagiarist," which is about a man who writes a novel riddled with plagiarisms, who then comes up with a bizarre strategy to prevent it from ever happening again.

"Terrific, Billy!" she said. "You certainly have a fertile imagination."

I laughed.

"But can I write?"

"Well, you can definitely learn. I have, and I've had less formal education than you."

I could hear the wheels spinning in her head.

Yes, I could actually hear the sound of Miss Mary Pickford thinking.

"Frances is coming next week to go over *Daddy-Long-Legs*. Why don't you sit in?"

To be honest, I was stunned by the idea.

Frances Marion was the most famous scenario writer in Hollywood!

Anywhere, in fact!

"Are you sure?"

"Sure, I'm sure, Billy. Frances won't mind. I'm sure of it."

As far as I could tell, except for Lilian Gish, Frances Marion was Mary's best friend. She was raised in San Francisco where she initially worked as a commercial artist. Then she took a job writing scenarios for Lois Weber Productions. When Mary offered her a position at Famous Players, Frances wrote the scenarios for *The Foundling*, *The Poor Little Rich Girl*, *Rebecca*, and others. When the war broke out, Frances went overseas as a war correspondent, and now that she was back from Europe, William Randolph Hearst was trying to lure her away to write for his Cosmopolitan Productions. Mary, of course, hated to lose her, but she always encouraged her friends to go wherever the money was waiting.

"Offers like Hearst's offer don't come along every day of the week," she'd told her friend.

So that's how it started.

Later that night Mary gave me a copy of Jean Webster's novel *Daddy-Long-Legs* which had been published seven years ago and was extremely popular.

Especially with young women.

It's about a young girl who's been raised in an orphanage and dreams of being a writer. When a trustee of the orphanage hears about the talented Judy Abbott, he offers to pay her way through college if she'll write him a letter once a month discussing her life and her educational development. He believes that letter writing is the best training for a young writer. (My mother certainly agrees with that, and I write her a detailed letter every two weeks, which she shares with my old man.) According to the arrangement, Judy's benefactor remains completely anonymous and never responds to her letters. She calls him Daddy-Long-Legs because she once saw his tall shadow at the orphanage.

The novel is written in a sequence of letters that Judy writes during her four years at college. Eventually, she tracks down her benefactor and they fall in love.

Naturally!

Mary loved the story so much that she wrote an adapted scenario during a four-hour train ride last November with some help from Agnes Johnston.

When I finished reading the novel, she asked me what I thought.

I did my best.

"It'll need more action and drama for a film, and I have to admit, I was a bit uncomfortable with the way that Pendleton seemed to manipulate Judy over the years. She's talented, spirited, and independent, and I feel that the love story needs to be more appropriate to her character."

Mary looked at me directly.

With the Mary Pickford stare.

"Exactly."

That was that.

If it was a test, I figured that I'd passed. Later that night she gave me a copy of her adapted scenario.

Now it was time to go over it with Frances.

With me!

I'm certainly not the nervous type, but I was definitely nervous about this little get-together. Mostly, I intended to keep my mouth shut.

The ladies sat on the couch, drank morning tea, then chatted about friends whom I'd never heard of. I sat nearby in a chair, feeling like an idiot.

Fortunately, the chatter didn't last too long.

"All right, my dear," Mary said to Frances, "we can gossip later. Let's talk about *Daddy*."

Which they did.

Occasionally, one of them would ask the ranch hand what he thought about this or that.

Like, "Do you think the prune revolt goes on too long?"

To which I offered, "Not at all. We need to see Judy's leadership and her fighting spirit. We also need the humor."

Which seemed to fly pretty well with the two Hollywood legends.

When we were done, Mary looked over at me.

"Final comments?"

"Well, I love the scene where Judy is playing the lead in *Romeo and Juliet*, and she can't remember her lines. I can only wonder where *that* came from."

Which I knew had already happened to Mary many years ago on the stage somewhere.

The ladies laughed.

Mary was always willing to poke fun at herself.

As for me, I learned a lot that day.

About structure. About the visual expression of character emotion and character motivations. About the proper use of humor within a serious story. About overall plot design. About all kinds of stuff.

I spent four hours that morning learning how to write.

After Frances left, Mary looked at me directly.

"Was that helpful, Billy?"

"Yes, ma'am, extremely."

She was pleased and smiled.

"Then we'll do it again. I'm thinking of doing a film version of Julie Lippmann's novel *Burkeses Amy*. I'll probably hire Bernie McConville to adapt it, and you can sit in on our script conferences."

Which is how, for better or worse, I learned to write.

Hearing stories as a child.
Reading my father's books.
Writing letters to my mom.
And learning from Mary Pickford.

8. Maternal Charities

Friday, February 7, 1919

"Who were *you* with last night?"

Mary spoke with an air of amused suspicion from the back of the Packard.

I hadn't told her I was going out with Wendy last night, and I'm not sure why I didn't tell her.

"How do you know I was out with someone last night?" I kidded back.

"The perfume, Billy boy. The perfume. I'd know that scent anywhere."

Well, whatever the scent was, it sure smelled nice when I was out with Wendy, especially when I held her close when I dropped her off at the Huntington Hotel in Pasadena."

Mary didn't let me off the hook.

"Did you kiss her?" she teased.

"Not yet, but it's on my agenda."

Twenty minutes later, Mary was sitting with Charlie Chaplin at a press conference inside the Maternal Charities auditorium. Mary really didn't want to be there, and she really didn't like Chaplin at all. She found him tiresome, moody, self-absorbed, and especially pretentious about politics, but she was "stuck" with him. Not only were they the two biggest film stars in the world, but he was also one of Doug Fairbanks's best friends. Maybe the best. The two men liked to hang out together and clown around together, so Mary put up with it. After all, she was in love with Douglas, and he worshipped the ground she walked on.

Now, of course, Mary was also a business partner with the both of them, and she and Chaplin had already supported a few charities together, including Maternal Charities on Sunset. It was a foundation dedicated to helping young single mothers, especially when violence had made their lives even more difficult. Today's case was especially tragic. A young mother, Suzanne Smith, who was sitting between Mary and Chaplin, had recently had her child kidnapped. The press was all over it, superseding the murders of Philip and Bonnie Burke, and Mary and Chaplin and the young mother were there to meet with the press and appeal for the child's return.

Suzanne Smith, totally distraught, begged for compassion, begging for her child to be returned. She seemed to be about my age, and she wore a nondescript black dress. She was clearly broken. She had large dark eyes, sultry with sadness, and long dark black hair. Several times she broke down, and Mary had to put her arm around the young woman to comfort her.

The message was simple.

"Please give me my child back."

Despite the distasteful involvement of Chaplin, Mary was always willing to help out with Maternal Charities, and, in this particular case, it was almost imperative.

The missing child's name was Mary Pickford Smith, and the fact that the mother had named her child in honor of the famous movie star had made the press even more interested in the abduction.

When Miss Smith (there was never any mention of the child's father) finished her short appeal, Chaplin reiterated her plea to the kidnappers, and he even offered a reward.

Mary did the same.

Apparently, there'd been no ransom demand so far.

I must say, standing at the back of the room behind the press, I was quite uncomfortable with Chaplin's role in all of this. It was well-known around town that he had an eye for very young girls, that he'd gotten several "in trouble," and that he didn't necessarily treat them right. I had no first-hand knowledge of any of this, but it was generally rumored around town, and his involvement with Maternal Charities seemed creepily inappropriate. Maybe his own behavior was the reason that he'd decided to support this particular charity.

Who knows?

As the press's question-and-answer session was winding down, Maurice Spector, who was well-known as a dirt-digging reporter for the *Evening Herald*, stood up and addressed a question to Mary.

Or was it an accusation?

"Miss Pickford, I wonder what Owen Moore is up to these days?"

He was clearly fishing.

Owen Moore was Mary's estranged husband, and it seemed that Spector was hoping for a reaction of some kind.

Mary seemed unaffected.

"Owen is currently working on an adaption of P. G. Wodehouse's novel *Piccadilly Jim*, to be directed by Wesley Ruggles and starring Zena Keefe."

It was a simple statement of fact, and most of the audience accepted it that way, but I knew that Spector was up to something, and I was certain that Mary did as well.

[Billy, I think you need to introduce me a bit. It's not 1919 anymore, and you're assuming that your readers will know my background, etc. I don't mean anything elaborate (please don't overdo it!) but help your readers to know who your co-detective is.]

As absurd as it seems (at least to me), I've been advised to give a few brief facts about Mary Pickford's life up until 1919. It seems to me a bit like explaining Queen Victoria to the English public or Annie Oakley to American citizens, but here goes:

I'll be succinct.

Mary Pickford was born Gladys Louise Smith in her home at 175 University Avenue in Toronto, Canada. She was the oldest of three children. When Mary was a young girl, her father John Charles Smith, abandoned the family, leaving her mother Charlotte, a talented seamstress, to try and support the family on her own. It was extremely difficult, and any hope that John Charles, an alcoholic, might return some day was soon dashed when he died from a blood clot after a work-related accident.

Strapped for money, Charlotte reluctantly agreed to

let her oldest daughter (age five) appear in child roles at the Princess theater in Toronto. Soon Mary's salaries were supporting the family, and eventually she took to the road, appearing in child roles in various plays around the country. It was a very hard life, but Mary enjoyed the acting, and she eventually got hired by David Belasco, the "Pope of Broadway," to perform in *The Warrens of Virginia* on Broadway. Mary was now fifteen, and Belasco changed her name to Mary Pickford.

Two years later, again needing money, Mary reluctantly agreed to seek work in the disreputable new world of cinema. Being a "Belasco actress," she immediately sought out DW Griffith who gave her an audition and supposedly said, with remarkable understatement, "I think you'll do." Very quickly, Mary became Biograph's top star, attracting interest all over the world. In 1911, she secretly married fellow Biograph actor, Owen Moore. She told me that it was the first time that she'd ever gone against her beloved mother's wishes, and she still regrets it to this day.

Mary made about 150 shorts (over 100 for Griffith), then moved into features with Adolph Zukor. In 1914, when she was twenty-two years old, she appeared in *Heart's Adrift* and *Tess of the Storm Country*, and had become, without question, the most popular actress in the world, as well as the most well-known female in the world, and the most admired.

The "Queen of the Movies."

Mary had an almost mesmerizing talent for playing appealing, charming, plucky, moral young women (sometimes young girls), and her many huge pictures over the past two years include *The Poor Little Rich*

Girl, *Rebecca of Sunnybrook Farm*, *A Little Princess*, and *Stella Maris*. All films which were widely admired throughout the world.

When the trouble in Europe started up, she was initially wary of US involvement, but after the *Lusitania* was sunk and the eventual US declaration of war, Mary put her considerable efforts into supporting the Expeditionary Force with propaganda films and cross-country tours raising money for the war effort. She was greeted with huge crowds everywhere she went, and at one stop in Chicago, she sold over five million dollars' worth of Liberty Bonds.

These are just a few biographical facts.

What of the woman herself?

(My boss.)

She is, like her reputation, ambitious, hard-working, and headstrong. She's equally kind, funny, empathetic, and charitable. She has no pretentiousness regarding her exalted status, fully aware that it can come to an end at any time. (Quite possibly whenever her love affair with Douglas Fairbanks becomes public knowledge.) She's as loyal to her fans as they are to her, and she does what she does out of a sense of duty. Invariably, she sympathizes and identifies with the poor and the downtrodden.

Especially orphans.

Especially mothers struggling as her mother had once struggled.

There's are many reasons why Mary is "America's Sweetheart." There's all her hard work, her dedication to her craft, and her desire to please her audience, but most of all it's because she *really is* a sweetheart in real life, and it comes through magically on the screen.

Trust me.
I know.

45

9. Griffith Park

Friday, February 7, 1919

"**What do you** want, Owen?"

Mary said it with a certain weariness that was definitely atypical, but she'd been putting up with this guy for the past eight years, and she wasn't about to waste any more time.

He hesitated.

He clearly didn't appreciate the fact that I was standing next to the both of them and listening in.

Right where Mary wanted me to be.

I think he was afraid of me, and I was fine with that. The guy was a mediocre actor on his way to becoming a full-blown drunk. He was also an abusive husband, and Mary had had enough years ago. He was a petty man who was jealous of his wife's success, and he'd bullied her not only emotionally but physically, even though she was barely five feet tall.

The first time I met the guy I gave him a look, and he knew exactly what it meant. If there was ever any ugliness, I'd kick his face in. In truth, I'm not really a hyper-aggressive type, but there's one thing I can't tolerate and that's men who bully women.

We were currently standing in marvelous Griffith Park in the late and overcast afternoon. Despite its name, the park had nothing to do with the great film director DW Griffith. It was actually named for some guy named Griffith J. Griffith who'd once owned an ostrich farm right here. (Yes, ostriches!) Then he donated over three thousand acres to the city of Los Angeles. That was twenty-three years ago, not long before he was convicted of shooting his wife in 1903. (Fortunately, she survived.) Both Griffith and his ostriches were soon forgotten, but the park is still beautiful. One of my favorite places in town. It's restful and lush and green, with ponds and streams and hills and California skies.

But this afternoon, the presence of Owen Moore ruined the place for me. Finally, when it was clear that I wasn't leaving them alone, he looked back at Mary.

"I'm being blackmailed."

Which meant that he wanted money.

I certainly wasn't buying his blackmail bit.

"By whom?" I asked.

Mary didn't seem to mind me butting in.

"Some bitch who's threatening to release my letters to the press. They insinuate a promise of marriage."

"Insinuate?" I said with disgust.

Moore looked directly at Mary and played his card.

"It would be bad press for the both of us, Mary."

Of course. *That* was this afternoon's manipulation. Give me some money or you'll be blackened in the press.

Mary just shook her head. She'd been dealing with this idiot ever since the day they met at Griffith's Biograph studio in New York City. Ever since she ran off with the guy and got married in a secret ceremony in New Jersey. Then right after the ceremony, she went back to her apartment and didn't tell her mother what she'd done, spending her wedding night alone in her bed.

Her biggest regret.

"How much?" she asked.

"Three thousand would put an end to it."

Pathetic.

The guy was a working actor, usually getting jobs because of his connection to Mary, but he invariably blew his money on booze, gambling, mistresses, and the so-called fast life.

Mary, prepared as always, pulled out her checkbook and wrote him a check. I never saw the amount, but I wouldn't be surprised if it was five thousand. Anything to get rid of the guy for a while.

Moore took his check, nodded at Mary, never looked at me, and walked away.

Out of sight.

When he was gone, Mary walked over to a little white wooden bench and sat down. Normally, she was inexhaustible, but Moore had a way of wearing her out.

I sat on the bench beside her and kept my silence.

"Douglas wants to marry me, Billy, and I want to marry him, but it would mean a divorce."

Mary had a habit of telling me lots of surprisingly personal stuff, but she'd never before talked about her failed marriage or her relationship with Douglas Fairbanks, the swashbuckling handsome movie star who, along with Chaplin and Mary and Will S. Hart, was one of the most famous film stars in the world.

From the little I'd observed, it was clear that

Fairbanks was crazy for Mary, but the question was whether the public would have trouble with "America's Sweetheart" getting a divorce.

"It could end my career," she said softly.

"It might not," I tried. "Americans love a love story."

She smiled.

"Frances thinks it's fifty/fifty," she added, meaning her close friend Frances Marion.

"Well, I think it's more like ninety/ten that it won't make a dent in your popularity, and I'm a paying customer. On the other hand, I'm just the guy who drives your car around."

She laughed.

I wish all those millions of people who go to her movies every week could actually hear her laugh. They'd love her even more than they already do.

Mary changed the subject.

"By the way, what did you make of Suzanne Smith?" meaning the young woman whose baby had been abducted.

"It's terrible, Mary, tragic."

It was the best I could do.

Mary nodded, but she still seemed wary.

"I don't know, Billy, I thought something was off."

"Off?"

"Yes, but I can't quite put my finger on it."

I was surprised.

"Do you think she's faking?"

"I don't know if I'd go that far, but something about the whole thing didn't feel right."

Then she looked over at me directly.

"But we'll have to leave it be, Billy. We've got two

murders to solve."

She said it like she might have said, "We've got some crossword puzzles to solve." She said it like the word "murder" was entirely unintimidating. Simply something to unravel.

She looked at me intently.

"Did you see him, Billy?" she asked.

"Who?"

"That young man standing in the back of the auditorium not very far from you. He wasn't with the press, and he slipped out before everything ended."

I felt like an idiot.

"No, I didn't see him. Do you think he's the same guy who was outside the Burkes' cottage in the taxi yesterday?"

"I don't know, Billy, but he definitely looked out of place at Maternal Charities.

"Do you think he's following us?"

She shrugged.

"Who knows? Maybe it's nothing."

Maybe it wasn't.

But it was clearly time for me to start getting a lot more observant if I was going to keep up with Mary Pickford and try to help her out.

"I'll keep my eyes open from now on," I assured her.

"Me too," she agreed.

Then we stood up and took the path beneath the trees back to the Packard.

10. Babylon

Friday, February 7, 1919

"Open your eyes!"

She did, and they blew up huge.

Then she kissed me quickly and looked around in wonder.

We were standing at the foot of a huge wide staircase lined with lion statues and Babylonian gods, surrounded by massive columns with gigantic white plaster elephants standing on top. It was the abandoned set on Sunset Drive for DW Griffith's three-and-a-half-hour epic.

Intolerance.

Wendy's favorite movie.

"I can't believe it!" she said, speaking in hushed tones.

Yes, the old set was abandoned just like an old ghost town, with weeds coming up in unwanted places amid the ruins, but it was still magnificent. This is where Griffith filmed Belshazzar's lavish feast with more than four thousand extras at the ridiculous cost of $250,000.

Which was just one sequence in the long movie!

Which cost more than twice the entire budget for *The Birth of a Nation*.

Which took place in the Babylon section of the massive epic that was composed of four interlocking narratives from different time periods throughout history:

> The fall of Babylon
> The death of Jesus in Palestine
> The St. Bartholomew's Day Massacre of the French Huguenots in 1572
> And a modern story about the clash between industrialists and their workers

After the extraordinary success of *The Birth of a Nation*, Griffith was offended by the justified criticism of his Southern bias and racial stereotypes. Raised in Kentucky by a former Colonel in the Confederate Army, Griffith was blind to his own biases, and he made *Intolerance* as a response to all the criticism. But the film was much too complicated for most audiences, and it failed badly at the box office. *The Birth of a Nation*, whatever its flaws, was a recognized masterpiece, and it made over twenty million dollars, which made Griffith an extremely wealthy man. But then he spent over four hundred thousand of his own money on *Intolerance*, and he ended up bankrupt.

There's no denying that the film was extraordinary on many levels, and Wendy loved it and had seen it five times.

Earlier, when I picked her up at the Huntington, I told her that I had a "surprise."

She was pleased.

"I love surprises!"

When I parked on Sunset Drive, I told her that she needed to close her eyes, and she agreed, as I guided her onto the deserted lot.

"It's amazing, Billy!"

We wandered around for a while and talked about the movie. She especially liked Mae Marsh's performance in the film, who'd starred in the contemporary narrative.

"Mary agrees," I assured her. "She was greatly impressed with Marsh's performance as the Dear One."

Eventually, we sat down on the wide staircase, and I asked her about herself. She confided that she's recently been hurt badly by a messed-up romance, but that she was getting over it. The guy, like a lot of guys, was a worthless bully.

She even cried a bit.

Finally, she took my hand and looked into my eyes.

"He wasn't faithful, Billy," she said softly.

Then she kissed me again like she believed that I was someone who could be both faithful and loyal.

Maybe I was.

I think I was falling in love with the girl!

11. Frank's François Café

Saturday, February 8, 1919

"Come along, Billy."

Mary had just finished an early lunch with Adolph Zukor at the new restaurant at 6669 Hollywood Boulevard. Frank's François Café. The place had already become popular with the Hollywood crowd, especially actors and executives.

Zukor, of course, was as big as an executive could be in this town, and despite his "business" divorce from Mary, they were still close friends.

Confidants.

As close as thieves over the Spanish omelet (Zukor) and the chef's salad (Mary).

I waited nearby at the long wooden bar and enjoyed a club sandwich.

Then Kaplan, Zukor's lawyer, showed up with some big thug-looking guy in a brown suit. I later learned that he was Aaron Sloan, a former LA cop, who was now Zukor's studio detective at Paramount.

Which meant that he was an enforcer.

Adolph Zukor did his best to keep his hands clean, and he was always gentle with Mary, but he wasn't afraid to use some muscle when needed. With troublesome actors. With troublesome theater owners. Etc.

Kaplan and Sloan walked over to Zukor's table, nodded politely at Mary, and waited. Then Zukor looked over at Mary, "Let's go somewhere private."

The restaurant wasn't packed, but it was busy enough, and it was well-known that its owner, Firmin Frank Toulet, kept a special room in the back for more private conversations.

Zukor had obviously reserved the room in advance.

As everyone headed toward the door at the back of the restaurant, Mary looked over at me.

"Come along, Billy."

I was surprised, but I did as I was told and followed along. Inside the back room, Mary, Zukor, and Kaplan sat at the wooden table, but Sloan, like me, remained standing.

Then he looked over at me.

He wasn't happy.

"What are you doing here?"

Mary spoke up immediately.

"He's with me."

Zukor nodded, and that was the end of that.

Once it was settled, Mary looked across the table at Zukor and got right to the point.

"So, what's this about a will?"

I had no idea what she was talking about.

Zukor looked at Kaplan who responded to Mary.

"It seems that Mr. Burke filed a Last Will and Testament with some local storefront lawyer a few weeks ago. The lawyer, a hack named Cortez, was instructed to send a copy of the will to Miss Mary

Pickford at the death of Mr. Burke. Since Cortez assumed that you were still working for Mr. Zukor, he sent the will to Paramount yesterday."

Kaplan, like the high-priced lawyer that he was, spoke the facts clearly and succinctly, but I sensed an underlying edginess that seemed to make no sense.

Mary prodded him.

"Well?"

"Everything's been left to you, Miss Pickford."

She was naturally astonished.

"Me?"

"Yes."

"Not his wife?"

Who was still alive when Burke had made out his will.

"No, not his wife."

Mary seemed as confused as I was.

"And what exactly is 'everything'?"

"All his capital and all his possessions, which, as far as I can see, adds up to very little. His rental home contained few worthwhile possessions, and his joint bank account with his now-deceased wife is about thirty dollars."

Kaplan slid the will across the table to Mary. It was a single page, with not much on it, with a bunch of signatures down at the bottom. I know nothing about such things, but it seemed odd that a married man's will would be so slight. It was like a two-sentence obituary.

Mary read it over quickly then looked at Zukor.

"Do you know what's going on?"

"No, Mary, I don't."

"Did you ever meet the man?"

"No."

"But you had him fired."

Zukor took it right in stride.

"Kauffman told me that he had an employee with a drinking problem in his finance office, so I told him to get rid of him. To be honest, I had no idea why Kauffman had bothered me about it in the first place, and I was rather irritated."

"Kaufmann implied that the order came from you. Or from someone at Paramount."

Zukor was surprised but not offended. He looked over at Kaplan.

"Do you know anything about this?"

"Nothing."

I wasn't sure if I believed him.

Zukor looked at Mary.

"How do you know these people?"

He meant the Burkes, both of whom were now dead.

"I met them at Biograph. Briefly. Then, as you know, the husband died on my property, and I discovered his dead wife in their cottage after his burial at Forest Lawn."

None of this made any sense to either one of them.

"There's something else, Mary," Zukor said, looking at Kaplan again.

We all waited.

Kaplan held up a small key and looked at Mary.

"There's apparently a safety deposit box at Commercial Bank on Melrose. Whatever's inside is yours. Would you like me to secure it on Monday?"

"No, I'll go myself," Mary said, and she held out her hand.

Kaplan gave her the key.

Reluctantly, it seemed to me.

Zukor changed the subject.

"Have they identified the child, Mary?"

"No, not yet, and there's no record of the Burkes ever having a child."

"What will happen to it?"

"Maternity Charities has taken the baby, and Mrs. Hilder will arrange for adoption if no one claims the little boy."

"Do we even know its name?"

"No."

Zukor was clearly concerned.

There was silence in the room.

"Is that everything?" Mary asked.

"No."

Now Zukor was even more concerned.

He looked at Mary like a worried father.

"An anonymous note turned up earlier today at the office," he explained. "It was addressed to me, but inside, it was clearly for you. It was unsigned and addressed to "MP" at the top of the page. The message was four words. 'Destroy it or else.'"

"Destroy what?" Mary wondered.

"I don't know, Mary, but I don't like it. Maybe it has something to do with Burke's deposit box."

Kaplan slid the note across the table, and Mary looked it over. Then she looked back at Zukor.

"Do you have any idea what's going on?"

"No, I don't."

I believed him.

"But," Zukor continued, "I'm worried about *you*, Mary. Since you're currently in between pictures and still recuperating from Influenza, I think you should leave town for a while. Maybe take a few days in Santa Barbara or somewhere else."

Mary thought it over.

"Maybe you're right," she agreed.

But I knew it wasn't that simple.

Mary wasn't one to back down from threats, and she definitely wasn't about to give up on the Burke murders.

I wondered what was coming next, and I was ready to go!

[Billy, I know I keep pestering you about background, but I think some more information about Adolph and DW and Mr. Belasco would help your readers. What do you think?]

In case you're not sure about some of the major players in Mary's life, here are three very short and inadequate bios:

David Belasco: The most important theatrical producer and impresario on Broadway for over thirty years. Known as the "Pope of Broadway." A proponent of natural acting and spectacular staging. He gave young Gladys Smith her first role on Broadway and renamed her "Mary Pickford." She once admitted, "To me, David Belasco was like the King of England, Julius Caesar, and Napoleon rolled into one."

DW Griffith: Without question, the most important filmmaker alive. He developed early cinema with over five hundred shorts that were seen and admired all around the world, some featuring Mary Pickford, Lilian Gish, Florence Lawrence, and many others. He and Mary sometimes had a contentious relationship, but underneath it all, I think that they truly loved each other. (And still do.) Eventually, Griffith moved into features and revolutionized the film industry (and film history) with his Civil War epic, *The Birth of a Nation*.

Adolph Zukor: Born in the Kingdom of Hungary, he emigrated to the US when he was sixteen years old. He became a wealthy furrier and entered the film business by investing in a string of movie theaters. Seven years ago, Zukor created Famous Players to make features, and four years later he merged with Jesse Lasky to create Famous Players-Lasky. Then he created Paramount Pictures to distribute his films. At the moment, I'd say that he's undoubtedly the most powerful person in Hollywood.

I hope that helps!

12. Occidental

Saturday, February 8, 1919

"Pull over, Billy."

I did as I was told.

Right in front of a huge building on North Street.

It looked abandoned.

"What is it?" I wondered.

"It's the old Hall of Letters building. It was once part of Occidental College before they moved to their new Eagle Rock campus a few years ago. I'm thinking of using the exterior for the orphanage in *Daddy-Long-Legs*."

It looked perfect to me.

It was a handsome redbrick in what I would later learn is Classical Revival style. It was easy to picture some of the scenes with young Judy Abbott and her orphan friends taking place right here.

But I did wonder about something else.

"What about the *real* orphanage?"

Mary was a generous trustee at the Los Angeles Orphan Asylum in Boyle Heights. She'd always had a special fondness for orphans, and she tried to visit the kids as often as possible. The place was run by the

Sisters of Charity, and it housed about three hundred young girls ranging in age from little infants to sixteen-year-olds. There were also a few boys, about twenty-five or so.

Mary always tried to keep her charitable donations anonymous, but given her celebrity it was often impossible, and her philanthropy was well-known in Hollywood.

She'd previously shot some scenes at the asylum for two of her previous pictures, *The Foundling* and *Stella Maris* (both written by Frances Marion), so I wondered why she was now thinking about the Hall of Letters.

Which was an entirely practical decision.

"The place is abandoned and easy to use, Billy," she explained. "Besides, I think it looks the part."

I certainly agreed.

In *Daddy-Long-Legs*, after Judy graduates from college she writes a book about orphans, obviously using her own childhood experiences (both the good and the bad) at the John Grier Orphanage where she grew up. I especially remember the telling line in the scenario, "for her soul is garbed in the hated gingham of the orphanage."

So what brought this on?

Why today?

It was an earlier visit to the Los Angeles County Jail.

To talk to Malaya Mendoza, the nurse arrested for her possible involvement in the kidnapping of the newborn child, Mary Pickford Smith.

Last night in Malibu, Mary called up Grayson and asked if he could arrange it. She wanted a brief meeting with the suspected nurse. Done in secret. With no publicity.

Grayson, of course, was a homicide detective, and he had no involvement with the kidnapping case, but he also had a lot of influence at the police department. Which was why Kaplan had called him four nights ago when Philip Burke was lying dead in Mary's Malibu garden.

I didn't hear the phone conversation, and I have no idea if Grayson thought it was a good idea, but he agreed to do it. Let's face it, it's hard to say no to Mary Pickford, and even harder to say no to Adolph Zukor, whom Grayson surely assumed had approved the idea.

At any rate, after Mary's meeting with Zukor at Frank's Café, we drove over to the jail house, and Grayson snuck us into a side entrance.

Into a little conference room.

No bigger than a jail cell.

Malaya Mendoza was waiting.

She looked crushed and hopeless.

She was a small woman, slightly plumpish, with a pleasant roundish face, which now looked terminally sad. As we already knew, she'd come to California from the Philippines as a young woman and worked in the maternity ward at St. Vincent Hospital. She was now thirty-eight years old.

Mary sat down facing the nurse.

Malaya was naturally surprised to see the famous actress sitting in front of her, but her sorrows mitigated any kind of normal response.

"Can I ask you a few questions?" Mary began gently.

"Of course, you can, Miss Pickford," Malaya

responded with excellent English with a marked Philippine accent. I guess she assumed that if someone like Mary Pickford had come to visit her in jail, it was unlikely to be an antagonistic visit, so she was ready to cooperate.

"Tell me about fifteen years ago."

Malaya nodded. It was clearly something that she'd rather not talk about, but she decided to do it for Mary.

As we already knew, Malaya had been arrested and convicted fifteen years ago for arranging an illegal adoption of an infant from the maternity ward at the Los Angeles Infirmary, as St. Vincent used to be known. As a result, she was sentenced to two years in prison, but due to certain "mitigating" circumstances (whatever that meant) the presiding judge reduced her sentence to two months in jail followed by a twenty-two-month probation. Malaya's nursing license was subsequently suspended for three years, but after it was reinstated, she was once again hired by the Infirmary to serve in its maternity ward. This was the same exact ward, now known as St. Vincent's, where Suzanne Smith had recently given birth to Mary Pickford Smith.

The next day, after Suzanne Smith returned to her apartment, her child went missing while she was sleeping.

But Mary wanted to start at the beginning fifteen years ago, and Malaya did her best to explain.

"The child had been abandoned and unclaimed at the hospital, and I knew of a young couple who were eager to adopt, so I tried to help them out."

"What did you do wrong?"

"I didn't follow the rules exactly, but I did nothing duplicitous."

"Why was it an issue?"

"There was an administrator at the time who had a problem with the Philippine nurses, and she turned me in to the police. It's true," Malaya admitted, "that I didn't fill out some of the required paperwork, but I was new to the position, and I wasn't aware of all the requirements. I suppose I should have known better, but abandoned babies were turned over to worthy couples all the time. It was the greatest joy of my life to work in that maternity ward."

"What became of the child?"

"It ended up with the exact same grateful couple. Everyone was happy but me."

I was now starting to understand the "mitigating" circumstances.

"When my license was renewed," she continued, "I was immediately rehired at the same hospital. In the exact same maternity ward."

"What about the problem administrator?"

"She was gone, thank goodness. Retired."

Malaya looked at Mary.

"You can ask anyone at the hospital about me. I'm not the kind of person who likes to speak highly of myself, but I'm a *very* good nurse. A very caring nurse. And I have many friends at the hospital. But now, for reasons that I can't understand, the nightmare has started all over again."

I must admit, she seemed perfectly believable.

Mary continued.

"Were you involved in the birth of Suzanne Smith's daughter?"

"Yes, I was actually in the room when the child was born, and I cared for the baby, along with a number of other newborns, later that night."

"Why do you think you've been arrested?"

"Because of what happened fifteen years ago."

"Did anyone working at the hospital accuse you of anything?"

"Not that I know of. Maybe one of the policemen realized that I was in the ward that night and made a false assumption. Or maybe it was a reporter. I really don't know, but I doubt it was anyone at the hospital."

Malaya looked directly at Mary.

"May I take your hands?"

It seemed an odd request to me, but Mary nodded, and Malaya took Mary's hands into her own.

"I would *never* do anything to hurt a child, and I've had *nothing* to do with whatever happened to Miss Smith's baby."

It was a direct appeal.

A powerful appeal.

"We'll see what we can do," Mary said.

Later when Grayson led us out into the daylight, Mary thanked him, and we got inside the Packard.

"Let's go over to North Street, Billy."

I headed in that direction.

"Did you believe her?" I asked.

"I did."

It was that simple.

13. Santa Ynez Canyon

Saturday, February 8, 1919

"There he is, Will."

We were standing in Santa Ynez Canyon beneath the oaks and the sycamores, near the fantastic sandstone formations and cliffs over the canyon's waterfall.

Less than an hour's drive from Los Angeles, the canyon is where Will S. Hart often filmed his westerns. Today he was working on something called *Wagon Tracks* about a trail guide (like Kit Carson) who leads a group westward along the Santa Fe Trail. The name of Will's character is Buckskin Hamilton, and he'd just finished a dangerous stunt on his horse Fritz over a narrow canyon trail.

When Will Hart heard that Mary was on location, he came right over. They were very good friends, which wasn't surprising since they were both easy to be friends with. Hart's popular films were always as realistic as he could make them, and he always played rugged characters with decency and integrity. It's true that he was just an actor, but he could actually ride and shoot very well, and he'd become an American

Western hero.

Then the two stars had a pleasant talk, with me listening in.

It was amazing how they'd both taken their fame in stride. How neither of them really had any interest in "being famous." In being recognized. In being idolized. The fact that they were was simply the result of their success as hard-working performers. I remember Mary's mother once telling me a story about Mary from years ago in New York City. She was riding on the subway, doing her best to be inconspicuous, when her little brother Jack asked her for a dime. When Mary refused, young Jack, being a clever little brat (still is) said that if Mary didn't give him what he wanted, he'd tell everyone in the subway car that she was "Little Mary," the star of all those Biograph films.

Mary gave him the dime.

Yes, Mary was now making over $200,000 a picture, over a million a year, and yes, over fifteen million people watched her films in the theater every single day of the year, but she remained, according to everyone who knew her, the exact same Mary.

Just like Will S. Hart.

Then Mary spotted what she was looking for. A bit actor named Royce Reynolds. He was an extra on *Wagon Tracks* and not looking very comfortable in his western outfit. He was also the guy who'd been hovering around Bonnie Burke at her husband's grave at Forest Lawn.

"I want to have a talk with him," Mary told me on the drive out to the canyon, "but let me talk to him alone at first. Then I'll wave you over when I need you. I want to get his trust first, and I don't want you intimidating him."

I was astonished.

"But I'm the most easy-going unintimidating guy in the entire Golden State!"

She laughed.

"You don't know what you are, Billy."

Maybe she was right.

Anyway, she said goodbye to Will then headed over toward Royce who was leaning against an old sycamore.

Which left me alone with Will, who was as kind to me as he'd always been.

Who had, as already mentioned, arranged for my driving job with Mary.

"Is she treating you well, Billy?" he kidded.

"Like a prince."

"And how's that shoulder of yours?"

"Close to mended."

"Well, if you ever need some wrangler work, just let me know."

Which I much appreciated.

As I kept an eye on Mary, our conversation continued for a bit until he had to get back to work.

He shook my hand.

"Take care of her, Billy."

"Yes, sir, day and night!"

He walked off, remounted his brown and white pinto, and rode off toward the film crew waiting near the waterfall.

Then Mary looked over in my direction and waved me over.

I walked toward the sycamore.

I guess she needed her "intimidator."

When Mary introduced us, we shook hands. Reynolds was a good looker, but he had a weak handshake, just like Chaplin.

A pretty boy.

Mary looked at me, then back at Reynolds.

"Royce wants to tell us about Bonnie Burke."

The guy was nervous and defensive.

"We were just friends, Miss Pickford," he insisted. "You know, actor friends. I met her at Biograph one time, and we talked a bit, and I liked her."

Even though I wasn't quite sure of my role in all this, I took a chance.

"Were you sleeping with her, Royce?"

Now the guy was really nervous.

"No, I wasn't! Absolutely not!"

He seemed convincing.

"Well, you seemed awfully solicitous at the cemetery," I pressed.

Maybe intimidators shouldn't use words like "solicitous."

"I liked her," he repeated, "and I felt sorry for her, and there was something 'off' about her husband."

Mary jumped in.

"What was 'off'?"

Reynolds tried to explain himself.

"I can't put a finger on it, Miss Pickford, but they didn't seem like a normal couple."

"Why? Because he was older?"

"I don't know. Maybe."

I jumped back in.

"Were there any problems that you knew about? Any rough stuff?"

"No, I never saw anything like that. They clearly

cared for each other, so maybe I was wrong about them, and now they're both dead anyway."

Which seemed to give him the creeps.

I continued to press.

"Did you think you had a chance with Bonnie once her husband was dead."

"Yeah, sure, I thought about it. She was a pretty girl, and I liked her a lot."

Mary nodded toward the canyon trail behind me, and I turned around to take a look. Detective Grayson and two uniformed cops were approaching in the hot California sun.

We waited.

I liked Grayson. I have to admit that given my old man's history with the Arizona Rangers, I'm partial to law enforcement types, and I felt that Grayson was both professional and capable that night in Malibu, as well as that afternoon at the Burkes' cottage.

Grayson nodded politely at Mary.

"Miss Pickford."

When she nodded back, he turned to Royce.

All business.

"You're under arrest, young man. Turn around."

Reynolds was terrified.

"What for?"

It seemed more like a little squeak than a question.

"The murder of Bonnie Burke, and possibly the murder of Philip Burke. Now turn yourself around."

Royce turned and one of the younger cops quickly cuffed him.

Grayson nodded at Mary again, then he led Reynolds away, down the dusty canyon trail.

Reynolds looked catatonic, but he continued

walking.

Guys with weak handshakes won't do too well in a prison cage.

"What do you think, Miss Mary?" I said suspiciously.

"I don't think he murdered anyone."

"That's what I'm thinking, too."

Then I thought I should check about something else.

"Did I open my mouth too much?"

Mary looked at me and smiled.

"You did just fine, Billy. We're in this together. All the way. Right?"

"Right! I'm your driver-detective," I kidded, describing myself.

"And I'm your actress-detective," she kidded right back, describing herself.

As we laughed at ourselves together.

14. LA Commercial

Sunday, February 9, 1919

I pulled out the deposit box.

It was Sunday, but when Mary showed up at the bank president's front door in Beverly Hills, the man was more than willing to take her to the bank and let her open her deposit box. Who wouldn't? How often does Mary Pickford show up at your front door?

I put the box on the table, and Mary opened it.

"It's like *Captain Kidd, Jr.,*" I said, and Mary laughed.

Just like the movie, we had no idea what was waiting inside.

Maybe nothing.

But there *was* something.

Something wrapped in a white towel.

Mary took it out and set it on the table. Then she opened it carefully.

There was a gun inside.

She was careful not to touch it.

She looked at me.

"Do you know what it is, Billy?"

"Yeah, it's a Smith & Wesson semi-automatic.

Model 1913.”

"Is it a good one?”

“Yes.”

“I think this gun has a history.”

“With fingerprints?”

“Maybe. Maybe that’s why it’s wrapped the way it is.”

I noticed something else.

“Look, there’s a wallet at the bottom of the box.”

Mary looked inside and took it out. It was old black leather and very thin. She opened it up. There was no money, just a single ID inside. A California driver’s license for Philip E. Campbell, 234 Hilcrest Drive, San Francisco.

“Maybe Mr. Burke wasn’t really Mr. Burke,” I said.

“Maybe not. Maybe something happened in San Francisco, and they left town together with bogus names.”

“And maybe that’s why there were so few possessions in their little cottage in Topanga Canyon.”

There was also a small slip of paper inside the wallet.

Mary opened it up and read it out loud.

“‘Please protect her!’”

Which was obviously written before his wife had been strangled to death.

Then the bank guy, an older man named Haliburton, came into the safety deposit room. He looked at the gun, but he didn’t say a word.

Instead, he looked at Mary.

“I checked it out for you, ma’am. That box was purchased three weeks ago by a man named Philip E. Campbell. He gave his address as 53 Topanga

Canyon."

Later, when we returned to El Matador, I went inside Mary's Malibu cottage to check things out. To make sure she'd be safe.

Holding my Colt revolver.

After all, Mary had clearly been threatened by that anonymous note that Zukor had passed along yesterday.

Anyway, there was no problem.

"Looks good," I called out.

Mary came inside. I think she thought I was being a bit over-protective, but she put up with me anyway.

"Are you ready for tomorrow, Billy?"

"I'm ready to go."

The phone rang. I didn't know if I should leave, so I stayed.

It was a quick call.

Mary put down the phone and looked over at me.

"The baby's missing."

I was confused.

"The baby we found at the Burkes' cottage?" I asked, still calling the Campbells the Burkes.

"Yes."

"Kidnapped?"

"Yes."

What the hell was going on?

15. Hippodrome

Sunday, February 9, 1919

I was watching the carousel go round and round.

With all the happy kids.

I was standing inside the Hippodrome on the Newcomb Pier, also known as Pleasure Pier, in Santa Monica. The odd Byzantine-styled Hippodrome was built by the Looffs to house one of their famous hand-carved carousels. Right here on the pier. Right over the ocean. Charles Looff had built the famous Coney Island carousel many years ago, as well as numerous amusement parks across the country. As well as popular "thrill" rides like Santa Monica's Blue Streak roller coaster, the Whip, and the Aeroscope.

The ornate carousel was much more tame, but today it was very busy with lots of families, lots of kids, lots of cotton candy, and all the rest of it.

Everyone seemed to be having a good time.

As for me, I was waiting for someone.

Mary was up the coast in Malibu, meeting with her favorite director to discuss her next picture, *Daddy-Long-Legs*. Marshall "Mickey" Neilan was a charmer who drank too much, but Mary loved him, and they worked well together. Mickey had directed some of her biggest pictures: *Rebecca of Sunnybrook Farm*, *The Little Princess*, and *Stella Maris*. Now they were getting ready for *Daddy-Long-Legs*, which was scheduled to start shooting a week from tomorrow on Monday, February 17.

Which meant that I had the evening all to myself.

I saw him approaching.

When I first saw Maurice Spector two days ago at Maternal Charities, the reporter was quite different than I'd expected. He was a slight little man with dark shiny hair and a pencil-thin moustache. He was probably about forty years old, and he looked more like a shady real estate dealer than a respected journalist. He worked for the *Evening Herald*, and he was famous around town for his numerous exposés of government corruption, especially in the mayor's office.

Now for some reason, he seemed interested in Mary Pickford and her husband Owen Moore. Which didn't make much sense to me, so I called his office and told him to meet me at the Hippodrome at five o'clock.

"Why should I? Who the hell are you?"

"Mary Pickford's driver."

That was more than enough.

"Fine, I'll meet you on the pier."

"I'll be wearing a dark suit with a red tie," I explained.

"Fine."

He hung up.

I think he thought I wanted to share something secret. Something salacious. Something that would get him and the *Herald* a lot more readers.

Gossip.

Maybe the guy was fed up with city politics. Maybe he wanted to get a bigger following, like that now-famous woman who wrote for the *Chicago Record Herald*. Her name was Louella Parsons, and she'd gone big time by writing a regular Hollywood "gossip column" that was syndicated across the country. In truth, it made sense. Who doesn't want to read "behind the scenes" stuff about all the Hollywood stars, especially their private lives?

Now I'd heard rumors that Louella Parsons was moving to LA, so maybe Spector wanted to plant his flag in the ground before she arrived.

The little guy walked right up to me, as confident as a man could be confident.

I didn't shake his hand.

Instead, I got right to it.

"Why are you bothering Miss Pickford about her husband?"

Spector was clearly disappointed, even irritated, to discover that I was here to *get* information and not *give* it, but he remained patient.

As well as forthright.

"You already know why, young man."

"I'm not sure that I do."

He thought it over.

"It seems that one of Moore's mistresses is blackmailing him."

I feigned shock as well as a non-actor ranch guy from Arizona was capable.

He seemed to buy it.

"What mistress?" I tried.

He smiled. Maybe he was thinking that I didn't

know anything, so he decided not to answer my question.

"It's a breach-of-promise threat," he explained, "which would be quite a problem for Miss Pickford."

"Is that what you want to do, Spector? Create a problem for Miss Pickford?"

"I want to publish the news before someone else does."

"Meaning Louella Parsons?"

He smiled again.

"Yeah, that woman already has spies all over my town, and it's rumored that she's moving out here herself."

"Does she know about the blackmail?"

"I don't think so."

"What would it take to make it go away?"

Meaning what would it take for Spector to forget about the whole thing.

"I have no idea. Something in return."

"Try me," I tried.

He thought it over.

"Does Mary Pickford know that you're here?"

"No."

Which was true. I was all alone in this, and I was hoping that I wouldn't make things worse.

"Are you really her driver?"

"Yes, as well as her confidant."

I'd clearly stepped over the line, but I felt that it was necessary.

"So, what could you offer me, kid? And don't tell me about Fairbanks. Everybody in this town knows about the two lovebirds, even though the public doesn't know about it yet."

Yeah, I always wondered about that. I figured that Zukor was somehow keeping a lid on it. Maybe his thug Sloan had paid a few visits to certain editors and certain reporters.

Who knows?

Maybe even Spector.

Who knows?

"How about stuff relating to her next project?"

"That sounds pretty lame."

"I could feed you interesting stuff before anyone else knows about it. Factual stuff that her fans would go crazy about, but nothing seamy."

He smiled at the word "seamy."

"You're a pretty nervy kid."

"I used to ride seventeen-hundred-pound bulls."

He laughed.

I think the guy liked me, and I sensed that he really wasn't as bad as I'd assumed. Maybe he really didn't want to be the kind of man who dug up dirt on movie people.

"All right, kid, I'll think about it."

He turned to walk away.

"What's her name?" I called out.

He knew exactly what I wanted.

It was the reason that I'd come to Pleasure Pier.

He turned around and shrugged.

"Why not?" he said to himself.

I waited.

"Arlene Addison."

16. Huntington Hotel

Sunday, February 9, 1919

I was sitting in the Horseshoe Garden.

I was early for my date, and I knew better than to knock on her door early. No woman wants that, right?

Nine miles from downtown LA, I was sitting in front of the elegant Huntington, killing time in the famous Horseshoe Garden, in the foothills of the San Gabriel Mountains in lovely Pasadena.

Henry Huntington, the famous railroad king, had bought this place (then known as the Wentworth Hotel) eight years ago, refurbished it, then renamed it after himself. Very quickly, it became an upscale retreat for the Hollywood elite and wealthy tourists.

I had no idea how Wendy could afford such a place since her most recent job was working as a receptionist at the now bankrupt Gold Coast Distributors in San Francisco.

Maybe there was money somewhere in her family.

I looked down at the red roses.

Six of them.

Her favorites.

I remembered that Mary once told me that when she

was a little girl, she actually ate some rose petals in the hope that she would become as beautiful as the roses.

"That's pretty weird, Miss Mary," I kidded her.

"Well, I was *very* little, Billy," she said, excusing herself with a smile.

Eventually, when the time was right, I walked up the outside stairs, toward the palatial façade, then into the reception area beneath its gilded ceiling and huge crystal chandelier.

When I knocked at Wendy's door on the hotel's first floor, there was no response. Nothing. I tried again. Nothing. Concerned, I went back to the reception desk and asked the concierge to give me a bellhop to open the door.

"I work for Mary Pickford," I told him, "and she's concerned about her friend."

Which, of course, wasn't true.

It was also a bit unethical to throw Mary's name around, but I was worried. Wendy was the punctual type, and I'd already seen two dead bodies in the past five days.

An eager-to-please bellboy, who was about my own age, accompanied me back to Room 123, opened the door, then waited silently in the doorway.

I stepped inside.

The room was spotless and empty.

No Wendy, no luggage, no possessions, no note, no nothing.

There was nothing left of her.

Just her lovely scent.

17. Hall of Records

Monday, February 10, 1919

"Look at this!"

We were going through the public tax and employment records inside the old Hall of Records in downtown San Francisco.

Mary looked over at me.

"Philip Campbell *wasn't* married," I explained. "He was actually a widower."

Mary was sitting behind her own pile of papers across the wooden table.

"So maybe they weren't husband and wife after all," she wondered. "Maybe they were father and daughter."

I'd never considered that before. Sure, Philip Campbell was a good bit older than Bonnie, but that happens sometimes, right?

"Were you suspicious?" I asked.

Mary smiled.

"It passed through my mind, Billy. In the cemetery the other day, Bonnie's grief seemed more like that of a daughter than a wife. It's hard to explain, and it was just a feeling that I had."

As you can see, it was hard to keep up with my fellow detective.

I shifted the subject a bit.

"How are you making out with Bonnie?"

Mary was searching for her tax records.

"Almost there."

Just like Philip, Bonnie had also worked at Gold Coast Distributors, where she knew Wendy Parker. On the long drive up the coast from LA, I finally told Mary about my dates with Wendy.

"Why didn't you tell me, Billy?"

"I don't know," I said honestly. "When I first met her at the cemetery, I thought that I might be able to get some useful information. After all, she said that she'd worked with Bonnie, and she was a good enough friend to attend Philip's burial. So I asked her out to the movies. One of yours, by the way. *Captain Kidd, Jr.* I was hoping to uncover some helpful information and then surprise you with it. But then something happened."

"What happened?"

"I started falling for you-know-who."

"Was my cowboy embarrassed about 'falling'?"

"I guess I was. I'd gotten nothing useful out of her, and I felt like the world's worst detective, so I thought to myself, 'Why does Mary need to know?'"

"Then she vanished."

"Exactly."

"You're quite the romantic," she kidded.

"Yeah, but usually girls don't dump me without a word."

She laughed.

"How do they usually dump you?"

"They don't," I said, maybe a bit too defensively.

But it was true.

Amused, Mary just shook her head.

"Well, I'm sure you got *something* out of her, Billy. Like her address in San Francisco. Or her phone number. Or something else."

"Nothing," I said sheepishly. "Just that she'd grown up in some place called Vallejo."

I guess I'd been played, but I'm not sure why. Her kisses certainly didn't seem fake.

Oh, well.

"You're not the first guy to fall for the wrong girl, Billy."

"Well, it's definitely the last time that's ever going to happen," I assured her.

"Famous last words," she said with a smile.

Then Mary settled deeper into the back seat of her Packard and went back to work, editing her *Daddy-Long-Legs* scenario.

The woman was always working.

She was never one to waste time.

"Here she is," she said in our isolated corner of the Hall of Records, "but her name wasn't Bonnie."

She peered closely at the files.

"Her name was Charlene Campbell. As of last year, she was listed as 'single,' and she'd filed returns for the previous year as well. She must have been sixteen when she started working at Gold Coast."

"The same year that Philip started."

Mary looked over at me.

"I think it's time to visit whatever's left of Gold Coast Distributors."

"Yes, ma'am!"

18. Gold Coast Distributors

Monday, February 10, 1919

The place on Mission Street looked totally deserted, but the front door was open.

When we went inside, guess who was sitting at the reception desk?

Maybe I should have been taken aback a bit, but I dealt with it both cool and collected. After all, I'd once ridden a monster named "Bloodshot."

I looked at Mary.

"Miss Pickford, I'd like to introduce you to Miss Wendy Parker, who kissed me twice one night on the set of *Intolerance*."

I looked at Wendy, who seemed a bit mortified.

"Well, Wendy, you once said that you'd love to meet Mary Pickford, so I brought her four hundred miles from Los Angeles."

Mary stepped forward, Wendy stood up respectfully, and they shook hands.

"Pardon Billy's manners, Miss Parker, but he's not used to getting dumped."

Wendy was dumbfounded.

I think that's the appropriate word.

Maybe flabbergasted would also work, but who uses that word anymore?

Mary continued, very businesslike.

"I'd like to speak in private."

Which seemed odd since the entire place seemed deserted.

Wendy nodded.

"Of course, Miss Pickford."

"Maybe in Mr. Durham's office?" Mary suggested.

David Durham was the now-deceased previous co-owner of Gold Coast Distributors. From what Mary and I could gather from the old news reports, the man had been shot in his office three months ago.

I had the distinct feeling that Wendy didn't like the idea, but she agreed anyway.

She wasn't about to say no to Mary Pickford.

Or to me.

"Of course," she repeated. "This way, Miss Pickford."

There was no mention of me.

We immediately followed her down a long empty corridor.

By the way, did I mention that she looked fantastic?

She was wearing a killer red dress, with a red ribbon in her long wavy thick blonde hair. She was a hundred percent All-American Girl.

On the drive from LA, after Mary had put away her scenario for *Daddy-Long-Legs*, she gave me a crash course in SF film history. I'd naturally assumed that there was no such thing, except for the countless theaters that every city in America had to screen Hollywood pictures.

"Actually," Mary explained, "back in the early

days, the Miles Brothers set up one of the first motion picture exchanges in the US, as well as the first studio on the West Coast."

I was astonished.

"Before Hollywood?"

"Yes, while we were still in New York."

"When was that?"

"About seventeen years ago. Initially, the four Miles brothers did some single-reel travel films, but then they started producing longer films of popular sporting events. Like prize fights. Like the lightweight bout between Jimmy Britt and Battling Nelson that took place in Colma, California, just south of San Francisco. But their most famous film was quite a bit different. It was called *A Trip Down Market Street*. Did you ever see it, Billy?"

"I did. Back in Tucson."

"The Miles brothers mounted a camera on a cable car, and audiences were fascinated to see the city unfold before their eyes as the cable car glided down Market Street."

"I remember it well. It seemed very unique back then."

"It was. That was back in 1905. Then the following year the earthquake put an end to everything, completely destroying the film business in San Francisco. Many of the local theaters were destroyed, many by the terrible fires in the earthquake's aftermath, and the Miles Brothers Studio burned down as well."

"So that was the end of it?"

"Pretty much, Billy. The city gradually rebuilt itself, including its movie theaters, but there was never much in the way of production."

"What about distribution?"

"Well, that's where Gold Coast comes in. It was set up about ten years ago to distribute films to northern California. It was always a bit of a nuisance for the Hollywood production companies."

"In what way?"

Mary just smiled.

"Let's just say that Hollywood likes to control everything."

I understood.

At Durham's office, we went inside and sat down. No one sat in Durham's chair behind the desk, as Mary and I looked around. It was a cluttered office, like many in Los Angeles, with no visible reminders of the murder that had taken place three months ago.

Wendy seemed a bit edgy. Which made sense. After all, her boss had been shot to death in this very room.

In that empty chair.

Mary looked over at Wendy.

"How well did you know Charlene?"

If Wendy was surprised that Mary knew that "Bonnie" was really Charlene, she didn't let on.

"We were friends, but just work-friends, so we didn't socialize out of the office, although I liked her a lot."

"Did you know that Philip Campbell was her father?"

"Yes, their deception and name changes took place after they left San Francisco."

"After the murder of Mr. Durham?"

"Yes."

"Why did they leave?"

"I have no idea. It was perfectly clear to the police that Mr. Martinez had killed Mr. Durham, so it made no sense to me when Charlene and her dad suddenly left town."

"How did you find them in LA?"

"It was a fluke. A coincidence. I was down in Los Angeles on business, and I went over to Biograph, and I ran into Philip."

"Then what happened?"

"He was perfectly pleasant, as always, and he took me over to their little cottage in Topanga Canyon. When I asked Charlene why they'd left so suddenly, and why they'd changed their names, she was pretty evasive about it. She said they wanted to start over. Start anew."

"Why?"

"She said that it had something to do with Philip's personal life back in their hometown, so I didn't press her about it."

"What hometown?"

"Amargosa."

Which I'd never heard of.

"How many times did you see her in LA?" Mary continued.

"Just that one time before the burial. She asked me not to mention anything about our lives back in San Francisco, so I assured her that I wouldn't. I felt sorry for her, and I was worried about her."

"Why? Did you think she was in danger?"

Wendy shrugged.

I've always liked her shrugs.

"Not really, but something was clearly wrong in their lives. Something that she didn't want to share."

"How did you learn about Philip's death?"

"When I called Charlene at the cottage. I had a few days left in Los Angeles, so I wanted to see her again before I headed home. When she answered the phone, she was completely distraught and could barely tell me what had happened."

"So you went to the cemetery."

"Yes."

"Where you met my Billy."

Wendy looked over at me, as if she was sorry that she'd left me staring at her empty room in the Huntington Hotel.

Holding red roses.

"Yes, where I met your Billy."

I suppose that was my opening.

"The roses I bought you are dead."

I meant it as a gentle jab.

"I'm sorry, Billy," she said.

She was getting a bit misty, but I wasn't sure if I was believing it.

Regardless, Mary didn't want things to get off track.

"You two can discuss your moribund romance later."

Which I thought was kind of funny, but Wendy didn't.

Then Mary got serious again.

"I want to talk," Mary said, "about what happened right here in this room."

It was perfectly clear that Wendy didn't want to, but she knew that she had to. Mary Pickford didn't drive four hundred miles to be put off by some untrustworthy receptionist.

"The LA newspapers," Mary began, "said that Carlos Martinez was a 'disgruntled employee.' Why was he disgruntled?"

"Because Mr. Durham fired him that day. It seems that Mr. Martinez's work was unsatisfactory."

"So he went and got a gun and shot his boss right here?"

"Yes."

Mary nodded across the desk.

"In that chair?"

"Yes."

"Did they ever find the gun?"

"Not that I'm aware."

Naturally, I thought of the gun wrapped in the towel in Philip Campbell's safety deposit bank.

I guess I've been a bit slow on the uptake.

Mary continued.

"Not even when they arrested the man at his house later that day?"

"Not as far as I know."

"What did Martinez do at Gold Coast?"

"He was a clerk. A numbers person. He worked in the finance department."

"Did you know him?"

"Only a bit. We'd nod at each other in the hallways. He was a quiet man, always polite."

"Were you here on the day of the murder?"

"I was. Sitting at my reception desk, when I heard the gunshot."

"Did you come here to the office?"

"No, I didn't. I let the men handle it. It was horrible, and I'd always liked Mr. Durham."

"Did you see Martinez leaving the building?"

"No, the police told us that he left through the back entrance."

Mary paused to think things over. Then she continued.

"Why is Gold Coast shutting down?"

"The buyout."

She said it as if she assumed that we knew about it.

"What buyout?" Mary asked.

"Mr. Durham and his partner Mr. Geller sold the company, and then the buyers shut it down. I'm the last one left on the payroll until the building is sold."

"I'd like to see the contract, Miss Parker."

"For the sale of Gold Coast?"

"Yes."

"One of the duplicates is still in Mr. Geller's old office."

"Could you get it?"

"Of course."

"And bring along another document with the signatures of both Mr. Durham and Mr. Geller."

Wendy nodded, stood up, and left the room. I'm sure that she was glad to get away from all of Mary's questions.

And just as glad to get away from me.

Mary looked over at her co-detective, who hadn't said much of anything.

"What do you think, Billy?"

"I don't know what to think. I guess I'm not sure how much we can trust her."

Mary nodded then got pensive again.

Soon Wendy was back, laying the legal document on the desk in front of Mary, who looked it over. Scrupulously. Mary Pickford was well-known in

Hollywood as a sharp businesswoman. Both she and her mother meticulously negotiated her film contracts, driving studio heads crazy with what would seem like minutia to ordinary people.

Mary looked over at Wendy.

"It's dated December 15th."

I didn't realize the significance at first.

"That's correct," Wendy agreed.

"That's the date of the murder."

"Yes, the contract was signed before Martinez did what he did."

Mary looked over at me.

"Come over here, Billy, and look at this."

I stood up and leaned over the desk. Mary pointed down at one of the primary signatures.

Howard S. Kaplan.

Of course!

Adolph Zukor had purchased Gold Coast!

Which made perfect sense. Paramount was the largest distributor in the world. Why wouldn't he buy out a smaller distributor in northern California? Especially one that was a pain in the neck.

I had the feeling that Mary had been suspicious of Paramount from the beginning.

But what did it mean?

Did it have something to do with the Durham murder that took place right here in this room?

Did it have something to do with the murders of Philip and Charlene Campbell in Los Angeles?

I wondered what Mary was thinking.

Then she took the other document that Wendy had brought along. It was a contract with an electrical company for services of some kind last year.

She lay the old contract next to the Kaplan contract, so that the signatures were right next to each other. Then she pointed down at the two Durham signatures. They were clearly not the same. Even I could see that.

I didn't say a word, but I was naturally wondering if Durham had been killed before someone had forged his name. Maybe he'd decided at the last minute that he didn't want to go through with the deal, so he was taken out of the picture and someone else signed his signature.

Which would mean that Carlos Martinez was innocent.

Mary collected the two documents and handed them back to Wendy.

Since Mary wasn't finished, I sat down in my chair again.

"Just a few more questions, Miss Parker."

"Of course."

I'm sure Wendy was wondering if these interrogations would ever end.

"How many men came from Paramount that day?"

"Two. The lawyer and another man."

"A big man?"

"Yes, very tough looking. I think he was wearing a holster under his coat, and I didn't like the looks of it."

Which sure sounded like Sloan.

Which also meant that Zukor wasn't here on the day of the signing.

"Was Philip Campbell here that day?"

"Yes, down in finance."

"With Martinez?"

"Yes."

"What about Charlene? Was she here that day?"

"Yes, she and her cousin were helping with the documents. Charlene was Mr. Durham's secretary."

"Who was her cousin?"

"Suzanne something. She was new at Gold Coast and assisting Mr. Geller."

"Was she pregnant?"

"Yes."

Wendy seemed as surprised by the question as I was by the answer. Apparently, Charlene Campbell and Suzanne Smith, the mother of the missing child, were cousins. Which seemed to reinforce my speculation from a few days ago that the baby found at the cottage in Topanga Canyon was actually the missing baby that the police were looking for.

Whoa!

Mary stood up and looked down at Wendy.

"You can now explain yourself."

Then Mary left the room.

So I sat there waiting, staring at Wendy, almost feeling sorry for her.

"I'm so sorry, Billy," she tried.

Naturally I wanted more than that, so Wendy tried again, attempting to explain.

"I didn't sleep at all the night before I left. I knew I was falling for you, Billy, but we lived too far apart, and we'd only been on two dates, and I thought that it made no sense. So I left the next day before you arrived."

It was pretty convincing.

Or was Wendy just a really good liar?

When I said nothing, she tried again.

"I thought about leaving you a note at the hotel desk, but I didn't know what to write. So I didn't. I just left. I was a coward, and I'm truly sorry, Billy."

"I'm a big boy, Wendy, and like you said, it was only two dates."

I stood up.

So did Wendy.

"I can't tell you," she said softly, "how much I care for you."

She went soft, leaned into me, and held me close.

I held her back. What else could I do? Besides, what man doesn't comfort a crying woman.

As always, I enjoyed her closeness.

Her warmth.

Her scent.

She looked up into my eyes.

I think she wanted to kiss me. Or for me to kiss her.

So I kissed her on the forehead.

Then I stepped back.

"No hard feelings, Wendy," I said. "I wish you nothing but good stuff."

Then I left the room thinking to myself, "That's one peculiar woman."

As well as, "That's one lovely woman!"

19. Palace Hotel

Monday, February 10, 1919

I was looking at the Pied Piper in the Pied Piper Bar in the elegant Palace Hotel, within the "new" Palace that had replaced the original hotel destroyed in the earthquake fire.

The Pied Piper, as always, was leading young children to their destruction.

It was very creepy.

The bartender told me that it had been painted by Max Parrish for the hotel's reopening after the 1906 earthquake.

It was huge, striking, colorful, and hanging above the long wooden bar.

I'm not really sure how it "fit in" with this upscale bar in the upscale Palace, with its luxurious Palm Court, marble lobby, and expensive suites.

After all, let's face it, the Pied Piper is an ugly manipulator and a child-killer.

Welcome to the Palace!

What would you like to drink?

As for me, I was sipping a Selzer thinking about another manipulator. Wendy Parker. I wasn't brooding.

All that was over and done. But I did wonder how much of what she'd told us earlier in the dead man's office was true.

On the drive over to the Palace, I asked Mary's opinion.

She laughed.

"Maybe eighty per cent. After all, Billy, most of it was factual stuff that others could have verified."

I nodded.

"What do *you* think?" she asked.

"Seventy percent."

She laughed again.

Like her smile, Mary has a warm comforting laugh.

Then someone approached me at the bar.

Who was not exactly a barrel of laughs.

He looked the same as he always did. Big, cold, tough. Wearing the same brown tieless suit. Who knows? Maybe he had a closet full of ugly brown suits back in LA.

Naturally, I was surprised to see him.

"What do you want?" I said, none too friendly.

"I'm here to see Miss Pickford."

"Why?"

"Because Mr. Zukor is worried about her."

He knew that any mention of his boss's name would get him what he wanted. Mary, as she usually did, had registered at the hotel under a different name. Everyone who saw her, of course, knew who she was, but she didn't want anyone at the front desk giving her room number to snoopy reporters.

Today she was registered as "Judy Abbott," the name of her character in *Daddy-Long-Legs*. As a result, Sloan had no idea what room she was in.

"Is she expecting you?" I asked, knowing that she wasn't. Given that Zukor had sent him, I also knew that I'd have to take this guy to Mary's room, but I didn't like him, so I made him wait a bit.

"No, she's not, but Mr. Zukor sent me."

I finished my seltzer.

Slowly.

Then I stood up straight.

I'm actually bigger than the guy, but he's much thicker. We'd be an interesting match, and I wondered if it might come to that eventually. The guy was afraid of nothing, and so was I. After all, I'd tangled with more than a few bullies at Camp Funston and out on the Rodeo circuit.

I looked him in his deadish eyes.

"Follow me, Sloan."

No "Mr." for him.

Upstairs, I knocked on 2015, and Mary opened the door and looked at Sloan.

"What do you want?" she said.

Which is exactly what I'd said.

He played his Zukor card.

"Mr. Zukor sent me."

She let us in.

We remained standing in Mary's lovely suite.

(As for me, I had a terrific single down the hall.)

Mary stared at the big creep.

"How can I help you?"

"Mr. Zukor sent me to see if I can help you."

Mary nodded over at me.

"I've got all the protection I need."

Which made me feel good.

Which also made me wonder if I was good enough.

I'd grown up on a ranch in Arizona, and I knew how to handle a gun better than anyone in the state of California, but I'd never been trained as a bodyguard. In truth, I had no idea what I was doing.

Sloan didn't comment on Mary's "protector."

"I also have some information," he added.

Mary waited.

"That actor's been released from custody. He was alibied by a young woman from somewhere up here."

He was talking about Royce Reynolds, whom Mary had never believed was involved in the Campbell murders.

I was more interested in the "young woman."

"What young woman?"

He didn't want to respond to me, but he did anyway.

"Some sketchy bimbo named Parker."

My Wendy trust-meter plummeted from seventy to zero.

"What else?" Mary prompted.

"Suzanne Smith has vanished, and so has all the money that you and Chaplin and that charity foundation raised to find her baby. Mr. Zukor wanted you to be prepared when you get back to Los Angeles."

"You can tell him that we'll be driving back tomorrow."

"I'm not sure that it's safe for you in LA. Maybe I should come along for the ride."

Mary immediately dismissed the idea.

"We'll be fine."

Sloan looked over at me.

"I'm not so sure about that."

"Well," she said, "I'm not at all interested in

whatever you might think."

That was the end of that.

Then Mary tried to dismiss the guy.

"Anything else?"

"Yes, Mr. Zukor thinks that I should accompany you to the bank when you get back home."

Obviously, he didn't know that we'd already been there yesterday.

"If I need your assistance, I'll contact Mr. Zukor," Mary said firmly.

Sloan just nodded.

What else could he do?

"Thank you for stopping by," Mary added.

She might as well have said, "Beat it, pal."

I walked over to the door and gladly held it open.

Sloan gave Mary his card.

"Call me if I can be of any help. I have some business in San Francisco tomorrow morning, and, like you, I expect to be back in Los Angeles tomorrow night."

Mary took his card and nodded politely.

When the big goon left the suite, I shut the door behind him.

I looked over at Mary.

There was no point in beating around the bush.

"Do you think he killed David Durham last December at Gold Coast?"

"I'm not sure yet, Billy."

"Do you think he killed the Campbells?"

"I don't know, but we're definitely going to find out."

If I knew one thing for sure, I knew *that* was true!

20. Hall of Justice

Tuesday, February 11, 1919

"Where *is* the gun?"

The defense lawyer looked directly at the SF detective sitting in the jury box.

"I repeat, Detective Stevens. Where *is* the gun?"

The lawyer for Carlos Martinez was grilling the lead detective on the Durham murder case. Mary and I were sitting in the back row of the crowded courtroom in the Hall of Justice.

Watching carefully.

The guy in the box looked flummoxed.

"We never found the weapon," he admitted weakly.

"Even though you tore apart Mr. Martinez's home."

"I wouldn't say 'tore apart,'" Stevens said defensively, "but we did give the place a thorough going over."

I looked over at Martinez sitting at the defense table, but I couldn't see him very well. He wore a grey suit and looked the picture of befuddled innocence.

"Let me summarize. As you've already admitted you have no witnesses to the crime."

"That's correct."

I almost felt sorry for the hapless detective.

"Similarly, you have no motive for the crime."

"As I said earlier, we were told at the crime scene by Mr. Geller that Mr. Durham had fired Mr. Martinez a few hours earlier."

The lawyer looked over at the captivated jury.

"Hearsay. Totally unreliable."

Then he turned back to the detective.

"Do you have any corroborating evidence of this so-called firing?"

"No, we do not."

Triumphant, the lawyer looked back at the jury.

"*There*, you've heard it direct from the lead detective. No weapon, no witness, no motive."

He looked at the judge.

"Nothing more from this witness, your Honor, but you might suggest that Detective Stevens return to his office and start actually solving this case since the *real* perpetrator is still out there somewhere."

The judge wasn't pleased.

"We'll have none of that, Mr. Norris!"

Norris nodded, and the judge continued.

"The witness is excused, and this seems a good time to take our lunch break."

Immediately, Mary and I stood up and left the courtroom. She was wearing a large dish hat with a shading brim and veil, but we were still concerned that she might be recognized.

Then mobbed.

I led her to a little conference room that I'd arranged earlier, and we waited for Norris.

It didn't take long.

Virgil Norris was a slight man in his forties,

although obviously tough in the courtroom. He wore a nicely tailored blue suit with a dark blue tie. He looked at Mary with astonishment even though I'd prepared him.

He stepped forward and politely took her hand.

"It's an honor, Miss Pickford."

He smiled, then he looked over at me.

"I honestly didn't know if your assistant was pulling my leg. It's not every day of the week that Mary Pickford asks to see an insignificant defense lawyer."

I liked him, so did Mary.

"No defense lawyer is insignificant," she said, "especially when his client is innocent, and I felt that you were very convincing in the courtroom."

Norris got a whole lot more serious.

"Well, I have to be. I'm certain that this jury is predisposed against us, and my client is definitely innocent."

I wasn't sure if he was referring to Martinez's status or his ethnicity. Were they bias against the man because he was a clerk who'd allegedly killed a powerful man of distinction and wealth? Or were they biased against him because he was Hispanic?

Maybe both.

"Are you sure about that?" Mary pressed. "After all, you probably say that about all of your clients."

"I have no doubt," Norris insisted. "Carlos has been framed. It's true that many if not most of my clients are guilty in one way or another, but not Mr. Martinez. Believe me, Miss Pickford, I'm being perfectly honest."

"We also believe that he's innocent," Mary said

flatly, getting right to the point, "and I wonder how long you expect the trial to last?"

It seemed an odd question, but Norris did his best to answer.

"Probably until the end of the week. Probably this Thursday the jury'll take over the case, and I expect them to decide rather quickly. Why are you interested, Miss Pickford? Do you know something I don't know?"

"I'm not certain who killed Mr. Durham, but I have reasons to believe that it wasn't Mr. Martinez."

"Can you share those reasons?"

"Not at the moment, but I wonder if you can delay the trial somehow and give me more time? At least until things go to the jury?"

He thought it over.

"I might be able to convince the judge to hold things over the weekend. Until Monday."

"Please do whatever you can. My assistant will call you if anything develops on our end."

Mary nodded over at me.

Her "assistant."

Mary stood up to leave.

"Can I ask," Norris asked, "how you got involved in all of this?"

It was a reasonable question.

"I'm afraid that I can't get into that right now."

He understood, and he didn't press.

"Thank you for any help you can give us," he said. "Carlos has a wife and two small children."

"We'll do our best, Mr. Norris."

Mary shook the man's hand, pulled down her veil again, and I held the door.

Soon we were driving south along the rugged Pacific coast to Montara.

The enormity of my responsibilities toward Miss Mary was really starting to weigh on me. She'd gotten herself involved in a complicated mess of crimes involving three murders, and I was the one responsible for her safety.

It was daunting.

Yet simple.

Protect the most famous woman in the world.

(And one of the nicest.)

21. Montara

Tuesday, February 11, 1919

The place was huge.

Monstrous, in fact.

Built with tons and tons of bucks.

Sitting on the coast of Half Moon Bay between the deep blue Pacific and the Santa Cruz Mountains.

Twenty miles south of San Francisco.

I pulled the Packard up the long driveway to the front of Geller's estate. The house looked like (from what I've seen in photographs) an English manor house. It was dark brick, three stories, with a dark hipped roof and turrets.

Yes, turrets.

A woman working in the garden told us that Mr. Geller was at the back of the house. I doubt that she would have told me anything if I wasn't standing next to Mary Pickford.

We strolled around the path to the back lawn and the wide ocean. Everything was beautiful.

Extraordinarily.

Gold Coast Distributors was in its death throes in downtown San Francisco, but the surviving partner who'd sold the company looked like he was doing just fine.

But, of course, looks can be deceiving.

He saw us as he was coming up the lawn from his dock and his yacht. He was a little guy, overweight, with thinning dark hair. He was wearing deck clothes in the bright California afternoon. He certainly didn't look like a mover-and-shaker, but then again, looks can be deceiving. Maybe he was a terror in corporate conference rooms.

He recognized Mary immediately, but he didn't seem to believe his eyes.

"Miss Pickford?"

"Yes."

She put out her hand, and he shook it gently.

"I wonder," she said, "if I could have a few words."

"Of course."

He led us over to his back patio, and Mary and I sat down in the comfortable chairs facing the ocean.

"Can I offer you anything?" he offered.

"No, thank you," Mary said politely. "We won't be taking much of your time."

He smiled.

"To be honest, I have nothing but time these days, and it's a pleasure to have you here."

"Have you benefitted from the Gold Coast sale as much as you would have wanted?" she asked.

It was a bit forward, and it took him aback a bit.

He got visibly cautious.

"Can I ask if you're here on behalf of Mr. Zukor?"

Geller had been in the film industry for at least a decade, and he obviously knew about the close relationship between Mary and Mr. Zukor.

"I'm not. I'm here on my own behalf."

Much relieved, Geller tried to answer her question.

"I did reasonably well in the buyout, but to be honest, other investments have left me in a rather bad place."

"Would you be willing to tell me about it?"

He rolled his eyes in frustration. Not at Mary, but at the world. The universe. Then he gestured at his manor house.

"I'm losing it all, Miss Pickford. I've already signed it over to an eager buyer. I know it seems hard to believe, sitting here in this lovely place, but I'm virtually bankrupt."

He seemed absolutely astonished by the fact, and more than a bit sorry for himself.

He looked directly at Mary.

"Oh, well, c'est la vie, right?"

"Just bad investments?" Mary asked.

"Yes, and I have to admit a good deal of overspending as well."

He looked down toward the dock and his yacht.

"Do you know what that thing is?"

"I have no idea," Mary admitted.

I had no idea either, but it sure looked impressive.

"It's called a Shipmaster. It's one of the largest motor-powered yachts in the world. Over a hundred feet long, with a twenty-foot beam, and 260 horsepower. Built by Consolidated Shipbuilding."

I'd heard of them.

They were big time.

"I won't tell you what it cost, Miss Pickford," he continued, "but I have to admit, it's my pride and joy, and I'm doing my best to hang onto it."

He laughed.

"I better. I'll be living in it soon!"

"Well, I bet it's very nice inside," I said stupidly.

Just like a kid.

(Hey, wait a minute! I *am* a kid!)

"Well, you're right about that, kid. It's even more comfortable than that big box behind us."

The big box behind us was the manor house.

Then Mary changed everything.

It was time to get serious.

"When will you be testifying in the Martinez case?"

We already knew the answer.

Geller paused nervously then answered.

"Tomorrow."

"Would you tell me what happened that day?"

He thought it over.

"Are you sure that Zukor didn't send you?"

"No, he didn't, but maybe Mr. Sloan did."

Which wasn't the case, but it sure made Geller pay attention. For a few moments, he just sat there and stared at his yacht.

"Just tell me the truth, Mr. Geller, then we'll leave you alone."

He finally decided that it was in his best interest. He certainly didn't want Sloan showing up at his home in Montara.

He shrugged.

"Well, the newspapers got it mostly right. We were in my office signing the transfer of ownership documents. When we finished, my partner David Durham shook hands with Mr. Kaplan and went to his office. A few moments later, while I was wrapping things up, we heard the gunshot, and we rushed to his office. It was horrible. Terrible!"

It was unclear whether Geller was telling the truth, but it was certain that he was greatly affected by the death of his business partner.

"Who else was in the room with you when the gunshot went off?"

"Mr. Kaplan, that guy Sloan, my assistant, and David's assistant."

"Meaning Charlene Campbell and her cousin Suzanne Smith?"

"Yes, that's right."

"Where was Wendy Parker?"

He shrugged again.

"At the reception desk, I assume."

"Did you know that Suzanne Smith was pregnant?"

Which seemed to come out of nowhere.

"Yes, but what's that got to do with anything?"

He was doing his best to conceal his frustrations.

Mary didn't care.

"Are you aware that both Philip Campbell and Charlene Campbell have been murdered?"

"Yes, it's terrible."

"Do you know why they left San Francisco the day after the murder of your partner David Durham?"

"No, but we *all* felt like getting away. It was a terrifying experience. A man had been killed. Murdered! A friend of mine!"

"Did you know Philip Campbell?"

"Not very well. David had hired him, and the man was down in the finance department most of the time. That's all I know, Miss Pickford, you can believe everything I'm telling you."

"Good, just a few more questions. About Carlos

Martinez."

Which made the guy really nervous.

To heighten his anxieties, I unbuttoned the front button on my coat and looked at him directly.

"You *better* be telling her the truth," I said.

Geller could see my shoulder holster and the butt of my Colt Service revolver.

As intended.

He got frightened, and I wondered if he was about to stand up and run away.

Instead, he looked back at Mary.

"Is that young man carrying a gun?"

"Yes, Mr. Geller, I've received a number of recent threats, and Mr. Kidd is fully prepared to protect me."

Geller was only slightly reassured as Mary continued.

"Are you planning to testify that Mr. Durham fired Mr. Martinez from his job on the day of the murder?"

It was clear that Geller didn't know how he should answer the question.

"I've been told," Mary pressed, "that you've informed the police that Mr. Durham had fired Carlos Martinez."

Geller did his best to cover himself.

"I told them what I'd heard."

"From whom?"

"From one of the girls, I think."

"Which one?"

"Think hard," I said with some threat in my voice.

"I really don't know. That whole day is a terrible blur in my mind. All I know is that I signed the transfer in my office, then we heard the gunshot."

"Do you think Mr. Martinez has been framed?"

"I wouldn't know about that, Miss Pickford, but I have no idea who else would have done it. In truth, I just wish it would all go away, and I'm dreading having to testify in court."

The guy was pathetic.

Mary stood up.

So did I.

She looked down at the frightened simpering man.

"Look at me, Mr. Geller," she said.

He did so.

"Was Mr. Sloan in your office when you heard the gunshot?"

"Yes, I believe he was. That's how I remember it."

"And who forged Mr. Durham's signature?"

"I have no idea what you're talking about."

I didn't believe him, and neither did Mary.

She turned around and walked away, but I stayed for a moment and glared down at the little creep.

He glanced up.

"I hope I won't have to come back here," I warned him.

He said nothing, but he definitely got the message.

It was fun playing the bad guy.

No wonder actors like acting.

Actually, I'm very easygoing and polite.

You can ask anyone.

22. Catalina

Tuesday, February 11, 1919

It was one of *those* parties.

When we got back to Malibu, there was a telegram waiting from Mary's younger sister Lottie, so we immediately drove to Long Beach and rented a boat.

Mary showed me the telegram:

> *Worried about J tonight. Hasn't slept. Off to Catalina with too much candy. – Lot*

Which I assume meant cocaine.

Jack was at it again.

Mary didn't mind either her younger brother or her younger sister having some fun, but their recent parties had created lots of talk around town about excessive booze, narcotics, and even "nudity." Whatever that meant. I'd been to lots of parties in LA, and I've never seen anyone walking around naked, but that was the gossip running around town.

Mary was less concerned about whether Jack and Lottie's Hollywood crowd had their clothes on than about Jack ending up in the hospital with alcohol and/or drug poisoning.

Even Lottie was concerned about tonight, so Jack really must be a mess.

This had happened many times before (with Lottie too), and Mary always ended up picking up the pieces. Tonight, she was all on her own since her mom was still in Toronto.

The parties on Catalina Island, far from the nuisance of LA cops, were especially infamous, and Mary was worried.

As for me, I didn't quite know what to make of Jack, whom Mary always called "Johnny." He was quite a likable guy, and supposedly he was a pretty good actor too, but he was unreliable, lazy, and aimless. A party boy. Even though he looked like a clean-cut "boy-next-door" type, Jack was clearly developing a serious drinking problem, and his marriage to former Ziegfeld girl and current actress, Olive Thomas, had exacerbated his problems. Like Mary herself had once done, Jack and Olive eloped to New Jersey for a secret marriage about three years ago, and the two of them had been acting like immature children ever since. Notorious fights, tearful patch-ups, and lots of parties and booze.

Lottie was more of the same.

Her talents were clearly the least of the Pickford children, and *Photoplay* had once called her "Pickford the Second," but she didn't seem to mind. These days her husband was out of the picture, and she was all about the Hollywood fast life.

So Mary, as always, had to be the adult.

As a result, Jack and Lottie bonded together, and they called Mary the "Policeman."

They also called her the "Czarina."

From what I've learned, they were always brats, and Mary, especially after their father had abandoned the family when she was five years old, had always done her best to help her mother by keeping her younger siblings in line.

But she wasn't always successful.

When they moved from poverty to enormous wealth, all of which was the result of Mary's hard work, Jack repaid her by getting girls pregnant, hanging out at clubs like Vernon's and the Sunset Inn, not to mention Tijuana whorehouses. Where he'd picked up the unsettling nickname "Mr. Syphilis." He also liked to gamble, managed to get a dishonorable discharge from the Navy, and, in general, led an aimless and dissipated life. With a little bit of acting here and there, all of which was the result of Mary's success and her many contacts in the business.

Another problem on top of all these problems was that Jack hated Doug Fairbanks, and Doug Fairbanks hated Jack.

Lottie, wherever she was tonight, was more of the same. Never as pretty as her older sister (how could she be?) and clearly limited as an actress, she seemed perfectly content with her reputation as an amoral sexually promiscuous young woman who preferred all-night parties to long days on Hollywood film sets.

So Mary did her best.

She was starring in one film after another, producing all of those films, running a production company, currently writing a new scenario, trying to solve three murders, and doing her best to keep her kid-brother and kid-sister out of trouble.

Out of jail.

So we stood on the deck of the small ferry heading into the Gulf of Santa Cruz.

Into the darkness.

After a very long day.

Which started at the Hall of Justice, then our stop in Montara with Geller, then the long drive down the coast to Malibu, then Long Beach.

I'd been to Catalina once before. It was lovely. Surrounded by the ocean beneath Mount Orizaba. It was also a privately-owned island, where all kinds of stuff could happen. (And did.) It was discovered by the famous Portuguese explorer Juan Rodriquez Cabrillo, who also claimed California for the Spanish Crown. It was once a haven for pirates and smugglers, but eventually it was set up as a resort community (Avalon) with a new pier and the famous Hotel Metropole. But a terrible fire four years ago along with the World War had decimated tourism, so now it was a safe haven for wild anything-goes parties.

Like tonight.

At the docks, I hired a driver to take us out to the party. Lucas Cain, the old guy at the wheel, didn't have to ask "which party," and he drove us straight to one of the old hotels on the southeast coast over the dark Pacific Ocean. The parking lot outside was jammed, and you could hear the music blasting from far away.

When we arrived, Al Jolson was singing "Rock-A-Bye Your Baby with a Dixie Melody."

Which sounded great to me!

But not tonight.

Tonight, I was the replacement "Policeman."

Mary, of course, didn't want to be seen at the party,

so it was up to me to go inside and somehow get Jack and bring him out to our waiting taxi.

No easy task.

It was now about 2:00 in the morning, and the place was in full swing. I won't attempt to describe the interior. Let's just say that every smoke-filled room was packed with pretty (often familiar) faces, with recordings blasting, wild dancing, hyper-loud conversations, confrontations, near fights, and vats of booze everywhere.

Fortunately, everyone still had their clothes on.

So far.

I saw lots of faces that you could see every week on your neighborhood theater screens.

Party girl Mabel Norman was dancing with Mary Miles Minter. I saw Roscoe Arbuckle and Chaplin sitting off in a corner by themselves. Etc.

It was a long way from Tucson.

But I was here for Jack Pickford.

Nothing else.

He smiled when he saw me. He was standing with some young actor named Valentino.

They held champagne glasses, and I saw no narcotics.

As already mentioned, I've always liked Jack. Whatever his flaws, the guy could be irresistibly charming.

Tonight, he seemed a bit unsteady on his feet.

"Well, I bet I know why you're here!" he said good-naturedly, slurring his words.

"I bet you do, Jack. She's outside."

"The Czarina is here!"

He seemed amazed by the idea.

He looked at Valentino and explained.

"The long arm of the law."

The young actor had no idea that Jack was referring to Mary Pickford.

Then, rather incongruously, Jack introduced us above the music and the racket.

"Rudy, this is Billy the Kid."

We all laughed, and I wondered how I was ever going to get him out of this madhouse.

I looked directly at Jack.

Real friendly like.

"Are we going to do this the easy way, Jack?"

Fortunately, he thought it was funny, and he thought things over.

"She's worried, Jack," I encouraged.

"Sure, Billy, why the hell not? I'm beat, and this place is dead anyway."

It sure looked pretty lively to me.

We nodded goodbye to Valentino and started slowly making our way through the crowded rooms. Jack, of course, had to say goodbye to everyone, which was very hard to do given how loud the music was.

I remember when we finally hit the front door, the Dixieland Jazz Band was playing "Skeleton Jangle."

As we approached the taxi, Mary hopped out of the back seat and looked down the dark road at a woman who was heading toward a waiting car.

Mary called out.

"Suzanne!"

I was astonished.

Was the missing mother of the missing child at a Hollywood bash on Catalina Island?

The distant woman ignored Mary and hopped in the

waiting car which immediately sped away.

"Was it really Suzanne Smith?" I asked.

"I think it was."

"Did you see who she was with?"

"No."

"Maybe we can catch her at the docks."

"Let's try, Billy," Mary said, as she reached for the door handle. Then a rifle shot went off and struck the car.

It was clearly intended for Mary.

Instinctively, I swarmed over her and drove her to the ground, trying not to crush her, waiting for a second shot. When I glanced up at Jack, he was still standing nearby staring down at his sister like an idiot.

Worried.

"Get down, Jack!" I yelled, and he seemed to snap out of it as the second shot struck the taxi's side window right above me. Jack immediately lowered himself, then rushed around the other side of the car. Safe for the moment. Hopefully, our old driver Lucas had safely ducked below his dashboard.

Fed up, I pulled my Colt, knelt in front of Mary and fired off four quick shots in the direction of the rifle shots. Firing into the thick dark woods near the old hotel. Since I couldn't see anyone, I fired high in the air in case any of the partiers were milling around outside the hotel, maybe having a smoke in the cool night air.

Nothing happened for a few moments, then I heard a powerboat race off from the far side of the hotel. I could see it faintly in the distance.

In the moonlight.

I stood up.

So did Mary.

"Did I crush you?" I asked.

"I'm fine, Billy, thank you. You did exactly what you needed to do."

Which was good to hear.

Mary Pickford with a broken arm (or any other injury) would have been a serious problem.

Obviously.

Then Jack came around the front of the car looking a bit sheepish, looking very concerned for the sister he loved, for the sister he invariably drove crazy.

"Are you all right, sis?" he asked.

He sounded like a little boy.

He'd also sobered up a bit.

"I'm all right, Johnny."

Then he came over and hugged her close.

It was nice to see.

Then he backed away and looked down at his famous sister.

"Why is somebody trying to kill you, Mary?" he asked.

"I don't know," she said. "Maybe they thought I was someone else."

It was curious watching Mary lie. She wasn't very good at it. Much too honest. But Jack didn't notice.

"Well, at least you're all right," he said, then he looked at me.

"Thanks, Billy."

I nodded.

I much appreciated it.

Fortunately, our driver was also unhurt and rather unfazed, but by the time we got to the Catalina docks, Suzanne Smith was long gone.

Assuming that it *was* Suzanne Smith.

Mary gave our old driver some cash for the bullet holes and the busted side window, and I wondered who had tried to shoot her as we waited to board the waiting ferry.

"Do you think someone followed us over here?"

Which seemed unlikely.

"I don't think so, Billy, and I also don't think that the telegram came from Lottie. I think it was sent to lure us out here to Catalina, where someone was waiting. Waiting for me to step out of the car."

Which made sense.

"We'll have to be much more careful, Miss Mary."

"You're right, Billy."

Then we stepped onto the deck of the small ferry along with party-wearied Jack and headed into the dark Pacific.

[Billy, I wonder if you were scared that night? You seemed so calm and collected. So was I, right? I've wondered about it sometimes, and I'm not sure why. Maybe it was because I'd been in so many similar situations in my films, and I'd reacted as I would have in the make-believe world of cinema? Who knows? Regardless, thank God for you, Billy boy!]

23. Purple Sage

Wednesday, February 12, 1919

Rise and shine!

It was a crack-of-dawn morning in my little cottage behind Mary's main cottage high above El Matador Beach in Malibu. I was already dressed and ready for the day, which was definitely going to be a long one.

Knock.

Who would be knocking on my door at this hour?

I opened the door.

"Hey, Billy," a fancy cowboy said with a smile, "you wanted to talk?"

Amazingly, it was Tom Mix, the famous film cowboy at Fox Studios, who really was a *real* cowboy, even though he didn't always look like it these days. Unlike Will Hart, who was all about realism in his films, and who always dressed like an everyday ranch hand, Tom's film characters were something quite different. Much flashier. Much more like you'd expect from a rodeo showman. Which audiences seemed to like a lot.

As previously mentioned, I'd first seen Tom when I was nine years old at Frontier Days Rodeo in Prescott,

Arizona, when he won trophies for both riding and roping. Five years later, I got to meet Tom when I won my first trophy in Prescott, and he generously took me under his wing with lots of good advice and good encouragement. Later, after the war and after the Spanish Flu, I started traveling with his 101 Ranch Rodeo tour based in northern Oklahoma. Then during an ill-fated show near LA in Covina, I got dumped by a seventeen-hundred-pound bull named "Death's Head" and wrecked my shoulder.

Which led to the army hospital, which led to Will S. Hart, which led to Mary.

This morning, Tom was wearing a white cowboy suit with red embroidery on the jacket and a white cowboy hat.

No ranch cowboy or herd cowboy ever looked like that!

"Look at that outfit!" I kidded.

He just laughed.

"It pays the bills, junior."

"Come on in, Tom."

As he did, as I was shutting the door behind us, I glanced over at the Model 66 Pierce-Arrow waiting in the dirt driveway. His driver was sitting up front, and there was some old boy slumped in the back seat, probably sleeping.

I didn't ask.

Tom sat down on my little couch, and I took a chair.

"You didn't need to come out here," I said.

"It's no problem, Billy, I was up in Ventura last night, and now I'm heading to Edendale to do some interiors."

I'd seen Tom several times since his visits to the army hospital while I was recuperating. He was currently shooting most of his next picture, *The Wilderness Trail*, out in Flagstaff, Arizona, but Fox preferred that he shoot his interiors in Edendale, where they'd created an amazing western set that was known around town as Mixville.

"How's your shoot going, Tom?"

"As well as it can, Billy."

"I hear you're working with Colleen Moore," I kidded. "Lucky you."

Tom has always had an eye for the ladies. He was thirty-nine years old, and he'd already been married four times.

"A perfect pleasure, Billy. She makes everything on the set go smoothly."

He looked at me directly.

We both knew that we couldn't sit around all morning shooting the breeze.

So he got right to it.

"What's up, Billy?"

"I wanted to ask you about an actress named Arlene Addison. She did some bits for you in *Western Blood* and *The Coming of the Law*."

He thought it over.

"Yeah, she's a young kid from California. With short dark hair, looking a bit like Colleen. I remember talking to her on a lunch break one time in Edendale. She told me that she had several horses in Covina, and she asked my permission to visit the Edendale stables. Since I couldn't take her myself, one of the grips gave her a tour. That's all I can remember."

"What did you think of her, Tom?"

"I liked her. She seemed like a nice kid."

He looked at me suspiciously.

"Is someone interested, Billy Boy?"

"I haven't even met her yet, Tom. I'm just wondering if she's an honest person."

"I didn't get to know her well enough, Billy, but she didn't seem like some of those young kids who'll do anything to get ahead. But what do I know?"

We thought it over.

"Does this have something to do with Mary?" he asked.

"More with Owen Moore," I said evasively.

He understood.

"I've never worked with that jerk, and I never will."

I nodded.

"Sorry that you stopped here just for that, Tom."

"Well, there's something else."

I waited.

"How's your shoulder?"

"Not bad, not great."

"Can you ride? I could use you on the Flagstaff shoot. I banged up my knee last week, and I need someone to double some of my stunts, so I thought of you."

Then, as if to qualify, he raised his hand.

"But I sure don't want Mary mad at me."

"I'm afraid I can't do it right now, Tom. Mary and I are wrapped up in something pretty intense, and she needs me."

He didn't pry.

"I understand, Billy. It was a long shot, but I thought it'd be fun to ride again in Arizona."

"I'd love to do it sometime. I really would!"

He stood up, and so did I.

"One more thing, Tom. Did you ever cross paths with a nobody actor named Royce Reynolds?"

"Nah, can't say that I have, Billy."

We exited the cottage, and he shook my hand.

"I'm a lucky man, Billy, but I miss the old times."

"There's nothing like a good bull ride."

"Nothing."

"By the way, I've got a suggestion."

"Tell me."

"Why not do a new version of *Riders of the Purple Sage*?"

He thought it over.

"Yeah, why not? Let me think about it." Then he looked over at the big cottage, "Give my love to Mary."

"I will."

I nodded over at his Pierce-Arrow.

"Is that who I think it is?"

"Yeah, you want to meet him?"

"I think I'll pass."

"Good, he's probably asleep anyway. Come down to Edendale and visit me whenever you can. We've got a hundred good horses in the stables."

"Sounds great, Tom."

I watched him walk to his car. With a slight limp. Like Will Hart, Tom did his own stunts, so he was constantly injuring himself.

He wouldn't have it any other way.

Then he got in the back seat with Wyatt Earp, and the Pierce-Arrow drove away.

Earp was in his seventies now, and he'd been doing some advising and consulting on a bunch of western films, and he'd become friends with both Tom Mix and

Will Hart. As well as John Ford. As for me, I was wary of the guy. My old man never really cared for him. He knew him from his cattle drive days in Kansas City and, of course, from his time in Tombstone, seventy-five miles from Big K Ranch. My old man knew a whole bunch of those old boys including Luke Short and Doc Holiday, and even Billy the Kid (whom he'd liked a lot) when the kid was living in Arizona before he went back to New Mexico and got caught up in the Lincoln County War.

Naturally, when I was a kid, I constantly pestered my old man about all of them, and he was always a good sport about it, giving me his honest impressions.

"What about Wyatt Earp?" I asked one time.

He shrugged.

"He always seemed on the make in one way or another. Doc Holiday actually enjoyed playing cards, but Wyatt took it way too seriously. Like everything else. He was always scheming about something or other. But I liked his older brother, Virgil. He seemed like a decent guy."

Oh, well, enough of that.

Time to see if Mary's ready to go.

Which, being Miss Punctual, she always is!

24. Fremont Place

Wednesday, February 12, 1919

Mary opened the front door, but I stepped inside first.

With my Colt ready.

The place was a wreck.

The place was Mary's modest little home which she shared with her mother Charlotte at 56 Freemont Place in the Wilshire District.

Charlotte, of course, was still in Toronto.

I turned to Mary.

"It's been tossed. Please stand over there."

I nodded at the corner of the tiny vestibule. I wanted to clear the house before she entered, and I certainly didn't want to leave her outside.

Exposed.

With my revolver ready, I checked out every room. The entire place had been ransacked, except for the kitchen and the bathrooms.

I went back to the living room.

"No one's here," I said.

Mary came inside and looked around. It was clear that someone was looking for something, and we both knew exactly what it was.

It was in Mary's pocketbook.

She smiled, calm as could be.

"Oh, well, we were planning to call Grayson anyway."

Which was true.

While Mary looked around at the mess, I called Detective Grayson, who said he'd come right over.

Mary was one of the wealthiest women in America, but her tastes were simple and traditional. Nothing showy, nothing look-at-me fancy, but everything was neat, meticulous, and well-made.

Eventually, she came back into the living room.

"Well, Billy boy, we're right in the middle of a big mess."

I knew what she meant. The mess wasn't her little house; it was the three murders.

The doorbell rang.

It was much too soon for Grayson.

"Stay back," I said, and she did what I asked.

It seemed highly unlikely that some kind of assassin would ring the front doorbell, but I was on extreme alert after last night's two rifle shots on Catalina Island.

I held the Colt behind my back and opened the door.

She was tiny.

Just like Mary.

"Is Mary at home," she said softly, as if she might have said, "Can Mary come out to play."

I was taken aback for a moment, which was peculiar these days. Working for Mary the past few months, I'd encountered all kinds of famous people, and I'd actually gotten quite used to it. Which is not to say that I still didn't enjoy meeting celebrities in the flesh, but it had become a fairly routine part of the job.

A welcome part of the job.

Now I was staring down at Mary's best friend, dressed in a simple green dress with green shoes and a small green hat.

She was probably the second most famous woman in the world.

"Yes, Miss Gish, please come inside."

I held the door open.

Lillian Gish was a year younger than Mary, and they'd met as child actresses when they were little girls, when Mary was still Gladys Smith. They even lived together for a while in the same flat on 39th Street in New York City when they were both looking for acting jobs. Similarly, they both had alcoholic fathers who'd abandoned their families. James Gish, however, unlike John Smith, didn't die soon after the abandonment. He ended up in the Oklahoma Hospital for the Insane. Both girls had loving devoted mothers who'd somehow managed to keep abject poverty from the door. Like Mary, Lillian had a younger sister, Dorothy.

It was Mary who'd introduced Lillian to DW Griffith, and when Mary left Biograph for Famous Players-Lasky, Lillian eventually became Griffith's favorite female star. Actually, his favorite star period. She was now world famous as the star of *The Birth of a Nation*, and the woman who "rocks the cradle" in *Intolerance*, and Marie Stephenson in *Hearts of the World*. Her next film, *Broken Blossoms* (an idea that Mary had suggested to Griffith) was due to come out sometime in the next few months.

I once asked Mary if she ever felt any regret about

leaving Griffith and forfeiting those roles.

"Not at all, Billy dear. Not as long as Lillian has taken my place. After all, I love her like a sister."

I stepped aside in the doorway so Miss Gish could come inside.

She looked at the mess around her, and she had the same astonished look on her face that I'd seen in many of her films.

"Mary! What have you gotten yourself into?"

Mary stepped forward with a smile, and they embraced like sisters.

"Oh, just some burglars, I guess. Who've obviously found out the hard way that all my money's in the bank downtown."

Lillian seemed somewhat reassured.

Somewhat.

Mary placed her pocketbook down on the table in the hallway, and she gave me a look. Then arm in arm, she and Miss Gish sat down on the couch in the midst of the clutter and started chattering away like schoolgirls.

Since Lillian had been off shooting *Broken Blossoms*, they hadn't seen each other in a while, and they had some catching up to do. Lillian wanted to know how Mary was feeling. Was she completely over the Spanish Flu? She also wanted to know how the scenario for *Daddy-Long-Legs* was coming along, and if she'd seen Frances Marion recently, and what was going on with Adolph Zukor.

As for Mary, she wanted to know how things had gone on the set with Griffith, and what her sister Dorothy was up to.

Etc.

I left them alone.

Surreptitiously, I stepped over to the hallway, removed the towel containing the Smith & Wesson, and went out the front door and sat down on the front steps.

Waiting for Grayson.

It didn't take long.

He arrived alone.

He looked the same as he always looked, serious but not unfriendly.

He walked to the front steps and sat down beside me.

"Let me take a look, kid," he said.

I handed it over.

Grayson set the towel in his lap and opened it carefully, exposing the semi-automatic. He was careful not to touch it.

"It's a Model 1913," he said routinely.

"It is," I agreed. "How long will it take to get some fingerprints?"

He looked over at me.

"Miss Pickford wants this on the down-low, correct?"

"Correct."

He nodded.

"Give me a few days."

"Fine."

"So I understand that you two think this gun killed some film guy up in San Francisco?"

"Correct."

"Fine."

Grayson looked up the street.

"Here come my boys."

A police car was approaching.

"Miss Mary's inside with Miss Gish," I explained.

He didn't bat an eye.

"Mary," I continued, "has told her friend that it's a simple burglary. Miss Gish knows nothing about our involvement with the two Burke murders."

Grayson still didn't know that the Burkes were really the Campbells.

He also didn't know about the rifle shots last night on Catalina Island.

"Fine. I'll keep it that way," he assured me.

The cop car pulled up at the curb with two uniformed policemen inside.

As they got out and headed for the door, Grayson looked over at me.

"I'm worried about you two, kid," he said.

He meant it.

I was worried too, but I put on a brave face.

"I can handle a gun," I offered.

"I hope so."

Then he stood up to greet his subordinates before they entered the house to search for evidence that might indicate who'd ransacked the place.

I felt certain that they'd find nothing.

So did Grayson.

25. Death Valley Junction

Wednesday, February 12, 1919

Love the name!

Hate the heat!

Not far from here, about six years ago, it actually hit 134 degrees, the hottest temperature ever recorded on the face of the earth.

Today was a balmy 104.

Actually, it was a melt-your-flesh 104.

Mary, of course, never complains about anything, and I'm not much for complaining either, so I guess we were well-suited for uncomfortable situations.

Earlier, we'd driven out to Death Valley Junction to see what we could learn about Suzanne Smith.

The young woman who was at Gold Coast when David Durham was shot.

Whose baby might or might not have been kidnapped.

Who might or might not have been kidnapped herself.

Who might or might not have absconded with the support funds provided by Maternal Charities.

Who might or might not have been at the party last night on Catalina Island.

Lots of "mights."

So we asked around the little town, which, these days, seemed more like a scattered settlement. D.V. Junction had once been created at a railroad spur to the borax mines in the mountains to the west. It's better known locally as Amargosa, and it's in the middle of nowhere.

In the broiling Mojave Desert.

The few people we found all directed us to the tiny home of Mrs. Irene Bedford, who was once the nearest neighbor of the Smiths.

She lived in a little white wooden oven, oops, I mean cottage, out on the flat desert in the blistering sun. She opened up the front door and looked at Mary Pickford.

Surprised to say the least!

Maybe she thought she was hallucinating. Can 104-degree heat make you hallucinate?

She stared at Mary.

"Is that really you?" she asked.

"Yes, Mary Pickford," Mary said, identifying herself.

"For real?"

"Yes, I'm Mary Pickford, and I was wondering if we might be able to talk for a bit."

What woman in America wouldn't say yes to that?

Mrs. Bedford collected herself.

"Of course, please come inside."

Mrs. Bedford was in her late-thirties, not unattractive, wearing a damp yellow housedress that clung tightly to her perspiring body. She had wavy damp dirty blond hair and curious green eyes. We'd already been informed by others in the Junction that she was a childless widow who lived alone.

We stepped inside.

It was hotter inside than it was outside.

Which seemed a physical impossibility.

The place was tiny but neat, with a few Southwest paintings on the wall intended to remind visitors that there was absolutely no escaping the Mojave Desert. There was also an empty gun rack on the wall.

"I'm sorry about the heat," she said.

I believed her, but even if it was ten degrees cooler, it still would have been hotter than hell.

(Did I say earlier that I'm not much of a complainer? Maybe I spoke too soon.)

She gestured to the couch, and Mary sat down.

Since I was an afterthought, I sat in an old rocking chair.

"Can I offer you some lemonade?" she asked.

"That would be lovely," Mary said gratefully.

A sweating glass pitcher was sitting on a nearby end table, and its ice cubes had already melted to the size of dimes.

I wondered if it would be appropriate to drink the entire pitcher in one gulp.

Mrs. Bedford took a step into her little kitchen, returned with two tumblers, and filled them both with lemonade. Then she handed one to Mary, and one to me.

Mine had none of the ever-vanishing ice cubes, but it was still a bit coolish and tasted great. I would have loved to ask for more, but I knew that I shouldn't.

On the couch, Mary just sipped at hers.

Ladylike.

Then Mrs. Bedford sat down next to Mary and stared at her directly.

Still in disbelief.

"It's hard to believe that you're really here in Death Valley," she said.

"We're glad to be here," Mary assured her. "We had a pleasant drive out from LA, and I'm very interested in what you can tell us about Suzanne Smith."

The widow thought it over.

"Suzanne left town about eight months ago. She was a month along."

We all knew what that meant.

"What was she like?"

"She was very pretty, very charming, but a bit uneven. She was also an exceptional athlete. She was actually the *entire* girls track team at our little high school down in Shoshone, participating in all the events, and she actually won the California State Championships all by herself!"

Which I found hard to believe, and I couldn't keep myself quiet.

"She competed against all the best teams in the state?" I interjected. "All by herself? And she won?"

I said it as politely as possible.

Mrs. Bedford was undaunted.

"Well, she didn't win every single event, young man, but she did win both the sprints and the hurdles, and she ended up winning the overall team championship. She put our little town on the map all by herself."

She seemed quite proud of the fact.

Mary tried to get things back on track after my intrusion.

"What do you mean 'uneven,' Mrs. Bedford?"

The widow thought it over.

"I not sure how to put it politely, but I think Suzanne is a bit unstable. She got into some fights with some of the other girls at school, and she even threw some rocks through the windows of one girl's home. Anyway, you get the idea. I don't like to be so negative, but I don't want to be deceptive either."

She seemed sincere enough.

"I appreciate that, Mrs. Bedford, and I wonder if you know who the father of her child might be?"

She nodded up and down.

Thoughtfully.

"Yes, I certainly do. My nephew Lloyd Garrison. They dated throughout high school, but when she got pregnant, she took off to live with relatives in San Francisco."

"What did her family think?"

"She had no family at the time. Her mom had raised her alone, but she died when Suzanne was sixteen."

"The girl lived all by herself?"

"Yes, she lived in the little rental house down the road, and I did my best to help out."

I did some figuring.

Since Suzanne was now eighteen years old, she must have been alone in that rental house for over a year before she took off for San Francisco.

"Is Lloyd still in the area?"

"Yes, he's over near Greenland Ranch. To be honest, I don't know what happened between the two of them, but it sure seemed like she just up-and-left one day without even telling him."

"Have you seen her since?"

"No."

"Has Lloyd?"

"Not as far as I know."

"What about Wendy Parker? Are you familiar with Wendy Parker?"

Mrs. Bedford thought it over, and Mary tried to help her out.

"Suzanne's cousin."

"I'm sorry. It doesn't ring a bell."

The widow looked over at my empty glass.

"Would you like some more lemonade, young man."

"I certainly would, thank you."

She poured it, and I drank it right down.

Mary gave me a look.

It was time to go.

When we stood up to leave, Mrs. Bedford looked at Mary as if the whole thing had been a dream.

A desert mirage.

"Could I shake your hand, Miss Pickford?" she asked, as if physical touch would somehow verify the reality of the visit.

"Of course," Mary said, and she shook the woman's hand warmly.

Mrs. Bedford looked into Mary's eyes.

"It gets lonely out here."

I bet it does.

"Take care of yourself, Mrs. Bedford, and thank you for your hospitality."

We went out the front door.

Into the Mojave again.

There was an old thermometer on Mrs. Bedford's front porch.

Things had cooled off a bit.

It was only 101.

26. Greenland Ranch

Wednesday, February 12, 1919

Borax.

"What *is* it?" I wondered.

Mary filled me in during the hot drive to Greenland Ranch.

"It's a salt, Billy."

"What's it used for?"

"It's used in hand soaps, and laundry detergents, and cleaning products, and lots of other stuff."

The "cleaning products" sounded a bit familiar.

"Anything else?"

"It's also used as a pesticide, like moth proofing, and it's even used in taxidermy."

I would learn later that the stuff was first discovered out here in Death Valley about forty years ago. It was initially mined by William Tell Coleman, who ran it out of the mountains then across the desert with his famous twenty-mule teams, until railroad spurs made them obsolete.

Mary was sitting up front with me in the Packard, as we drove along in mostly silence staring at the bizarre landscapes surrounding us. It was a truly amazing part of the world, with interminable salt flats, mountain-sized sand dunes, sandstone canyons, and the endless deadly Mojave. The area was inhabited by only a few brave souls: Timbisha Indians, the borax workers, and other assorted weirdos living in Furnace Creek, a speck of a town in Death Valley, which was first stumbled onto by lost and parched Forty-Niners.

We kept the car windows wide open, hoping for a breeze, but the hot dry desert air rushed into the Packard like a furnace blast. Regardless, it still seemed better than rolling up the windows and creating a four-wheeled sweat box.

Eventually, we stopped at old Greenland Ranch, a large adobe house that was once a key location in the Pacific Coast borax empire. Some old guys sitting up on the veranda directed us to Lloyd Garrison's little house down the road toward Badwater Basin, the hottest place on earth.

"Does he live alone?" Mary called out through the car window.

She was hidden well enough that the old miners didn't recognize her.

"Yes, he does, Missy, but I haven't seen him for a bit."

The others agreed with thoughtful nods.

Mary followed up.

"What does he do for a living?"

"He clerks over at the railroad spur."

It was now approaching sunset, so maybe Garrison would be home from work.

"Thank you," Mary called out, as I drove us away toward Badwater, and we soon found the isolated Garrison place on a long stretch of white desert.

"Don't park too close, Billy," Mary said.

I guess she wanted to surprise the guy.

I parked, and we got out of the Packard, and we looked around. There was nothing but Mojave in every direction. Nothing that resembled civilization.

Nothing slightly human.

"How do people survive out here?" I asked rhetorically.

Miss Mary, who knew lots of stuff about lots of stuff, just shrugged.

"I have no idea, Billy."

We looked over at Garrison's house.

It was a white wooden rectangular box with a faded red door and a small white awning.

Neatly kept.

Mary looked at me.

"He won't be happy to see us," she said.

"Why not?"

"Because he's probably got the baby inside."

I was astonished. Maybe I should have already made the connection.

The supposition.

"So you think he went down to LA and stole his own baby?" I said rather stupidly.

"I do, and I think he might have been the same young man who was standing in the back of the auditorium during the press conference at Maternal Charities."

I was catching on.

Slowly.

"Maybe," I speculated, "he was also the young man in the taxi outside the Campbell's cottage in Topanga Canyon?"

"Maybe. I wouldn't be surprised."

I took it even further.

"Do you think he murdered Charlene Campbell?"

"I don't know, Billy, but we need to be careful and approach him with caution. Hopefully, he hasn't seen us coming."

"Let me go in first," I said. "I'll get the drop on him."

Mary laughed her little laugh.

"I guess you really are a cowboy, Billy."

"Yeah," I said, "Billy the Kid!"

She laughed again. Then I got serious again.

"We can't have Mary Pickford shot dead in the Mojave Desert," I said. "Just let me take care of it."

She agreed.

Reluctantly.

Besides, maybe she was wrong about Lloyd Garrison, and the guy was all alone inside his little house.

I pulled my Colt and headed toward the little building.

The sun was setting in the distant desert, and the sky was streaked with orange above Telescope Peak and the Panamint Mountains. It looked a lot like the beautiful sunsets of my youth in southern Arizona.

Carefully, I made my way around the house and looked in all the windows. Each one was curtained, which seemed a bit odd. Even a bit ominous. At the rear of the house, I went up to the back door and turned the handle.

Silently.

It was unlocked.

I opened the door a bit and stepped carefully inside.

Slowly, I made my way down a short hallway toward the living room right into the barrel of a pump-action shotgun.

A Remington Model 10.

"Stay right there!"

The angry voice meant it, so I did as I was told.

The guy holding the shotgun was dead serious.

Garrison looked a bit older than me. He was tall like me, and he was quite athletic looking with trim dark hair. He was also a good-looking young man, a bit worn by the desert heat, who was clearly ready to blow my head off.

"Don't move that Colt," he warned me, so I didn't.

"What are you doing in my house?" he demanded.

It seemed like a fair question.

But I never got to answer.

"Lower that shotgun, young man."

It was a tiny female voice coming from behind Garrison somewhere. Mary had obviously come in the front door and was now standing right behind Garrison, hidden from my view.

From Garrison's as well.

"Now!" the little voice said firmly, so Garrison lowered his weapon. I quickly stepped forward and grabbed his shotgun. Then he turned around, and we both looked down at little Mary. She was holding a metal lipstick case in her hand. The cylindrical kind. She'd obviously pressed it into Garrison's back, and he thought it was a gun.

Didn't I once see Mary do something like that in one of her movies?

I wondered who felt like the bigger fool?

Me or Garrison?

Mary looked up at me and smiled.

"So who got 'the drop' on whom?" she kidded.

Seeing that it was Mary Pickford, Garrison relaxed a bit, even though he knew why she was standing in his little hot living room.

"Have a seat," I suggested, and Garrison sat down on his own couch.

I holstered my useless Colt then propped his Remington against the far wall. Mary sat down in a chair facing Garrison, and I sat in one next to the front door.

"Do you have the child?" she asked.

"What child?"

"Your child, of course. Mary Pickford Smith. Or should I say Mary Pickford Garrison?"

"I really don't know what you're talking about."

"Should I send Billy into the bedroom?"

Garrison shook his head.

In defeat.

The jig was up.

He tried to explain himself.

"Of course, I took my own baby back from its irresponsible mother! Who wouldn't?"

"I understand," Mary said, with a compassion that Garrison clearly appreciated.

"But why," Mary continued, "did Charlene Campbell end up with the child?"

He shrugged.

"Who knows? It seems that Suzanne simply dumped the baby in Topanga Canyon so she could run off and do other stuff."

"Like what?"

"I really don't know. Go to parties and get drunk, I

suppose."

He looked over at Mary.

"She wasn't always like this, Miss Pickford. Yeah, she was a bit flighty, I suppose, but she was never so self-centered and irresponsible. Back when her mom got sick, Suzie took care of her every single day. Better than any nurse could have. But when I got her pregnant, she went off the rails. She told me that she was going to visit her cousin in San Francisco, and she never came back."

"Never?"

"Never. But she sent me a postcard. She said that she'd decided to stay there for a while. And that was that. Nothing more."

"Do you still have that card?"

"No, I burned it."

"Did she say where she was staying?"

"Yeah, some place called Redlands, but I think she made it up. It's not on any map I've ever seen."

"So you went to San Francisco to look for her?" Mary prompted.

"Yes, but she was already gone. I guess the murder of her boss must have spooked her. Just like her cousin Charlene."

"How did you find her in Los Angeles?"

"It wasn't easy, but I knew that Charlene would be looking for acting work, so I hung around Triangle Studios for over a week. I figured that every out-of-town actor would eventually try to meet with DW Griffith, and I was right. One afternoon, I spotted her coming out of the main office in Culver City, and I followed her to her cottage in Topanga Canyon."

"And discovered the false names?"

"Exactly, and the fact that Charlene and her father were pretending to be a married couple, which seemed awfully peculiar to me. I guess they were involved in that murder up in San Francisco, but I wasn't interested in any of that. All I wanted was Suzanne. I knew that she must have delivered the baby by now."

"Did Charlene tell you where she was?"

"She said that she didn't know, and I believed her, and I was terribly discouraged. Then I saw an article in the *Evening Herald* about the kidnapping of our child. Naturally, I didn't believe it for a minute, but then I got worried that our baby was probably dead and would never be found. Finally, I decided to go back to Charlene and try to pressure her again, and when I got there, she was holding my baby."

"Suzanne had given it to her?"

"Actually, Suzanne secretly dumped the child into Charlene's house without a word. But Charlene had put two and two together, and she and her father were trying to figure out what to do. They certainly didn't want to go public and blow their covers. They were deathly afraid about that business up in San Francisco, and with good reason, I assume, since they both ended up dead."

"So, you made a deal?"

"Yeah, we made a deal. I would take the baby back here, and that would be the end of it. I told her I'd come back the next day to get little Mary, but when I arrived the police were there, and Charlene was dead, and the baby had been taken by Maternal Charities."

Mary looked at him directly.

"Did you kill Charlene Campbell?"

He seemed appalled by the question.

"Of course, not, Miss Pickford! Charlene was a lovely person, and she was trying to help me. I was devastated by her death."

"Do you know who killed her?"

"No, but I wish I did. I suspect it was some thug from San Francisco."

"Do you know anything more about what happened in San Francisco?"

"No, I kept out of it. I had other things on my mind, and Charlene clearly didn't want to talk about it."

So it looked like Lloyd Garrison wasn't going to be much help, and I'm sure Mary was as disappointed as I was, but she kept asking questions about the baby.

"Then you kidnapped the child from Maternal Charities?" she continued.

"Yes, if a man can be said to 'kidnap' his own child. I suppose I could have made a legal claim, but Suzanne was still out there somewhere, and I just wanted to take my baby home to Greenland and raise her properly."

I believed the guy, and I liked him. He'd clearly been through a lot.

He looked at Mary.

"Will you need to involve the police?"

He was begging, and I certainly didn't blame him.

"I don't think they need to be involved," Mary assured him.

His relief was palpable.

"Thanks so much, Miss Pickford. I had a very good father when I was a boy, and I want to be the same."

Mary stood up, and I did as well.

She looked down at Garrison who was still sitting on his couch.

"One more thing," she said.

Garrison stood up.

"Anything, Miss Pickford."

"I'd like to see the baby."

He smiled and quickly led us back to the bedroom, where he picked up the resting baby into his arms. He seemed like a natural.

Mary looked closely at her namesake.

"She looks like me," she kidded.

Garrison smiled.

"Would you like to hold her?"

"Yes."

Which she did so tenderly.

Then a few minutes later we were back driving across the darkened Mojave.

27. Paramount

Thursday, February 13, 1919

They call it the house that Zukor built.

Even though Mr. Zukor usually called it the house that Mary built.

Regardless, we drove through the main entrance on Melrose onto the Paramount lot. Everyone recognized Mary's blue Packard, and everyone waved. I wondered if she had any enemies in this world. I certainly didn't know of any. But she definitely had her likes and dislikes. I'd learned over the past few months that she wasn't very fond of Chaplin, DeMille, Goldwyn, and a few others, but these were just people that she found distasteful in one way or another.

Hardly enemies.

Nevertheless, two nights ago, someone had fired two rifle shots at Mary on Catalina Island, then someone had ransacked her house yesterday.

Regardless, I had the feeling that Mary felt safe on the Paramount lot. I suppose I felt the same way, but I still reminded myself to be on guard.

We parked and went directly to Mr. Zukor's office.

Mary immediately hugged the old boy, and Zukor

shook my hand like a gentleman. He didn't seem at all concerned that Mary's driver was "sitting in."

Whatever Mary wanted, Mary got.

What she wanted today was for both Kaplan and Sloan to be waiting for her in Zukor's office.

They were.

Uneasily.

Wishing they were somewhere else.

Anywhere else.

Politely, Kaplan shook hands with Mary, and Sloan nodded deferentially in her direction.

I was, of course, ignored, which was fine with me.

Once Mary had sat down in the chair facing Zukor's huge mahogany desk, the most powerful man in Hollywood sat down as well.

I sat off to the side.

Kaplan took the chair to Zukor's left, facing Mary, and Sloan stood against the far wall behind his bosses.

This should be interesting!

Mary looked at her old friend.

"Why didn't you tell me?"

"Tell you what?"

"That you bought out Gold Coast."

He seemed surprised, almost amused.

"Well, I'm trying to buy up *every* pain-in-the-ass distributor in the country. You already know that, Mary."

"Yes, but there was a murder at Gold Coast on the day that Mr. Kaplan finalized the buyout."

Zukor looked over at Kaplan.

"Is that true?"

"Yes, it is, sir," Kaplan confirmed, "but it had nothing to do with the transfer of ownership."

"You still should have told me, Howard."

"I'm sorry, Mr. Zukor."

He looked sorry.

He also looked like a man who was guilty of something.

Guilty of *lots* of somethings.

"I wonder *why* he didn't tell you," Mary continued, "especially since the man who was murdered was David Durham, the co-owner of Gold Coast, and especially given the fact that both Bonnie Burke and Philip Burke were there that day before they fled San Francisco, came to LA under aliases, and were subsequently murdered."

Zukor looked astonished, and I believed his astonishment.

He was also confused.

He gave Kaplan a cold look, then turned back to Mary.

"Should I have Sloan look into this?"

Mary shook her head.

"That would be something I definitely *wouldn't* want."

I looked over at Sloan who never flinched. He seemed imperturbable.

Zukor was clearly frustrated.

"What exactly do you want, Mary?"

"I want your lawyer to tell me what happened that day, and I want him to tell me the truth."

Zukor looked at Kaplan.

"Well?" he prompted.

Kaplan did his lawyerly best.

"After we signed the papers in Bryan Geller's office, his partner David Durham left for his own office. A few minutes later, we heard a gunshot, and when we got down to Durham's office, he was already dead. Shot through the heart, still sitting in the chair behind his desk. Geller immediately called the police, who eventually arrested some disgruntled employee, whom I believe is currently on trial for the murder at the Hall of Justice. That's it, sir. Everything. Since it didn't involve Paramount in any way, I didn't bother you about it. It would have seemed like gossip."

"Gossip! Someone was dead, Howard, and two more would end up dead!"

Z was furious, and Kaplan was humiliated, but Mary wasn't finished.

"Who was in Geller's office when the gunshot went off?"

"Geller, me, and Sloan," the lawyer answered, "and two of the Gold Coast secretaries."

Mary clarified for Zukor.

"Yes, one of whom was a young woman named Charlene Campbell, who immediately changed her name to Bonnie Burke, moved to Los Angeles, and was eventually strangled in her cottage in Topanga Canyon."

Now Zukor was even more astonished.

"That's not all," Mary continued. "Charlene's father Philip Campbell, who also worked at Gold Coast, was the same man who was shot to death and died in my garden in Malibu."

Now Zukor was totally confused.

Why wouldn't he be?

It *was* confusing.

"What am I supposed to make of all this, Mary?"

"I'm not sure myself, but I think Kaplan and that

guy leaning over on the wall over there know a lot more about this than they're telling you."

Zukor looked back at Kaplan, who defended himself.

"That's it, boss. I swear! We finalized the deal, and there was an unrelated shooting. Afterward, we gave our statements to the cops, and we got out of there right away and drove back to LA."

"Did you know that the girl strangled in Topanga was the same girl who was in Geller's office?"

"No, I had no idea. She was just someone in the room that day who was helping with the documents. I hardly noticed her."

"And her father?"

"I never met him, and I've never even heard of him. Whoever he was, he had absolutely nothing to do with the transfer of ownership."

"Speaking of the documents," Mary interjected, looking at Zukor, "do you have the ones I asked you about?"

"Of course."

Zukor opened a prepared folder on his desk, then he slid the contents over in front of Mary.

Mary waved me over, and I pulled my chair right next to hers so I could also see the document.

It was the transfer of ownership agreement. It seemed to be about ten pages or so, and Mary immediately turned to the last page, so we could look at the signatures together:

Bryan G. Geller
David Durham
Howard S. Kaplan (representing Paramount and

Adolph Zukor)

Witnessed by:

Charlene Campbell
Suzanne Smith
Aaron Sloan

Naturally, we looked closely at Durham's signature.
It was clearly forged.
Mary looked over at Sloan.
"I'd like a glass of water."
Which seemed to come out of nowhere.
The big guy didn't like being treated like a servant, but he did as he was asked. As everyone waited, he poured a small glass from the pitcher on Zukor's side table, then he brought it over to the desk and set it on a coaster right in front of Mary.
"Thank you," she said without bothering to look at him.
Then everyone watched as she took a sip.
Holding the glass at the bottom with her gloved right hand.
She was definitely acting again, and I wondered if the others knew it.
I don't think they did.
Then she looked directly at Kaplan.
"Mr. Durham's signature has been forged on this document. I've seen his actual signature on several other documents at Gold Coast."
Although clearly defensive and nervous, the lawyer did his best to be firm.
"I'm afraid you must be mistaken, Miss Pickford. I

witnessed David Durham sign his name to that document before he left the room. We all saw him sign it."

Zukor was furious.

"You better have seen it, Howard. If you didn't, it might void the buyout."

Kaplan looked directly at his boss.

"I saw him sign it, sir. I'm positive. He did so right in front of me."

Zukor looked back at Mary.

She looked back at Z.

The room went silent and tense and hot, and I was enjoying it quite a bit.

I guess actors know how to "take a beat" even in real life.

It was marvelous.

Then Mary looked directly at Zukor.

"I would like these two men to leave the room."

She said it with all the regal authority of Queen Victoria.

Of Catherine the Great.

Of Nefertiti of Egypt.

Zukor immediately waved his hand like the Queen's consort, and Kaplan stood up. Then he and Sloan slithered out of the room.

Without a word.

Without a look.

Z looked back at Mary.

"Do I need to fire those two idiots?"

"Not yet," she said, which didn't seem to bode well for the two "idiots."

"Good, because Kaplan's a hell of a lawyer."

Which made him think about legalities.

About not owning a company that he thought he owned and which he'd already put out of business.

"How sure," he asked, "are you about that signature?"

"Why don't we leave that be for now," Mary suggested evasively, which was fine with Zukor.

"Do you have the other things I requested?"

"Of course."

He slid over another file, and Mary opened it up. It contained various handwritten documents and notes and memoranda written by both Kaplan and Sloan. The one on top was a report about a theater strike that took place in San Jose two years ago. One that, if I remember correctly, was reputedly busted up by some of Zukor's goons.

Meaning Sloan.

"These are privileged documents," Zukor pointed out.

Mary ignored him and continued studying the documents.

I'm no handwriting expert and neither is Mary, but it was pretty easy to eliminate Kaplan's chicken scratch. On the other hand, it sure looked to me like Sloan had forged Durham's signature.

Zukor, of course, was one of the smartest men in Hollywood, and he knew exactly what Mary was doing.

"Did either one of them do it?"

Mary looked up, still in her evasive mode.

"Possibly."

Zukor seemed fine with "possibly." I had the feeling that he really didn't want to know if the transfer document was legally void. After all, Gold Coast Distributors was ancient history.

Mary closed the folder and looked at her friend.

Then she looked back at me.

"The pitcher, Billy."

I stood up, took hold of the water pitcher, and placed it on the table in front of her.

Zukor watched with bemused amusement.

Then Mary, holding her water glass at the bottom again, poured the water back into the pitcher. She was wearing the same immaculate cotton white gloves that she always wore when she was out of the house or off the set.

She held up the glass to the light.

We all could see Sloan's fingerprints.

Satisfied, Mary took a small scarf out of her pocketbook with her left hand, carefully wrapped the glass, and placed it safely inside her pocketbook.

She looked at Zukor.

"Thank you for the refreshment," she said with a smile.

The old guy laughed.

But he was still worried about her, and he looked over at me.

"Don't you let her out of your sight, kid."

"I won't." Then I tried to reassure him, "I grew up on a ranch in Arizona, and I know how to handle a gun."

I wasn't bragging, it was true.

"Well, I certainly hope it won't come to anything like that."

Which is why Mary never mentioned Catalina Island to Zukor.

Or to her mother, Charlotte.

Or to Fairbanks.

Or to anyone else.

Jack knew, of course, but Mary had sworn him to secrecy.

Z looked at M.

"Please be safe, Mary. You can be a bit headstrong."

Which she took as a compliment.

Mary stood up, and I did as well.

But Zukor wasn't finished.

"Maybe you should drop this, Mary. After all, you're just a little actress running around the state with a juvenile cowboy."

Mary smiled.

"But he's the best cowboy west of the Mississippi."

Zukor laughed, and Mary walked around the desk for their goodbye hug.

It seemed much longer than their other hugs.

Then it ended.

"I love you, Mary," Zukor said. "But you drive me crazy, and you worry me to death."

It was now Mary's turn to laugh.

"Oh, you'll forget me as soon as I walk out the door. You'll be cutting deals, and bullying competitors, and stealing star contracts."

"I'll be sitting at my desk worrying about you," he insisted.

"Good," she said, then she walked out the door.

Held open by her juvenile cowboy.

28. La Brea Tar Pits

Thursday, February 13, 1919

This was another kind of graveyard.

Quite different from Forest Lawn.

I was standing with Mary in the La Brea Tar Pits. For the past six years, archeologists had been digging all around the place searching for the fossils of old mammals. Like Columbian Mammoths, dire wolves, and saber-toothed cats.

Some of them 20,000 years old.

Supposedly.

I'd been out here once before, and I was told that, in the past, some sticky oily stuff seeped up from inside the earth and whenever animals would wander into the deadly pits, they'd get trapped. Then dumb predators would go in after them and get caught themselves. Eventually, the goop hardened into something called pitch or tar (or "brea" in Spanish). It all sounded rather disgusting to me, but it was apparently a scientific nirvana.

It was now just after four o'clock in the late afternoon, and all of the diggers were gone, and the entire eerie place was empty.

Which made it even stranger.

Even weirder.

An hour ago, Kaplan had called Mary in Malibu.

He wanted to meet.

Privately.

Mary suggested the tar pits. She'd shot some movie scenes nearby, and she figured it would be about as private as a place could be.

Nevertheless, I was on high alert.

As for Mary, normally she was indefatigable, but I'd nursed her through the flu a while back, and I'd seen her when her strength was down.

"Are you all right, Miss Mary?" I asked.

"I'm fine, Billy. Maybe a bit tired. I haven't been sleeping the best."

I wondered about nightmares.

Mary had once told me that she had two recurring nightmares.

In the first, she walked out on an empty stage to perform, and the theater was empty.

In the second, she walked out on the stage, and she forgot her lines, so she ran off the stage fully expecting to be fired.

I guess they were both indicative of her committed sense of duty about her career. After all, she'd begun acting on the stage when she was seven years old. I suppose the nightmares also said something about her compulsion to provide for her family. Her mother once told me that when Mary was still a child, she declared, "I'm the father in the family." Meaning the provider. Which she'd been doing her entire life.

"The same two nightmares?" I asked.

"No, Billy, a brand new one."

I waited.

"I'm in the bedroom of the cottage in Topanga Canyon, and I'm staring down at the strangled body of Charlene Campbell. But the dream is different from how it really happened. You weren't there, Billy, and I was all on my own, and when I touched her body, she moved."

"Whoa! What happened next?"

"I woke up! Thank goodness!"

"What do you make of it?"

"I guess we're supposed to find her killer."

"We will, Miss Mary," which I said with all the enthusiastic bravado of an overconfident youth.

[Yes, I still have those same nightmares on occasion. All three. But I guess I've grown accustomed to them by now. Oh, well, such is life!]

We saw him coming.

Howard Kaplan was one of the most powerful and feared lawyers in Los Angeles, but he always appeared slight and unthreatening, with a thin face and an innocuous pencil mustache. As usual, he wore an immaculately tailored blue suit and shiny black shoes.

He looked worried.

Very worried.

There was obviously a weight weighing on the man, and it seemed as though he was ready to reveal himself.

To unburden himself.

He nodded politely at Mary.

"Miss Mary," he said softly.

But Mary didn't shake his hand. The man had been

giving her the runaround, and she wanted answers.

Now!

It seemed that he was ready to begin.

"Just tell me the truth, Howard," she said.

"That's why I'm here."

Then he was dead.

Instantly.

A red splotch appeared at his forehead.

His head jerked back, and he collapsed like someone had pulled his plug.

Or cut his strings.

Immediately, I grabbed Mary and forced her down to the ground for the second time in the last two days. Fortunately, she's so tiny that I was able to cover her almost completely.

But she managed to force her way out from beneath me so she could crawl over to Kaplan. His eyes were fixed, as if astonished by his own sudden death.

"What did you do in San Francisco, Howard?" Mary asked pointlessly, but Kaplan was dead, and the dead tell no tales.

By now, I'd pulled out my Colt and was looking in the direction of the rifle shot. I could see nothing but endless tar pits. Then I heard a distant car drive off.

It was over.

I helped Mary to her feet.

I wondered if she'd be having a different nightmare later tonight.

The La Brea Tar Pits now had a new dead body.

I stared off in the direction of the fleeing car, but I could see nothing.

All I could think of was:

"Damn! That was a hell of an impressive shot!"

29. Marina del Rey

Thursday, February 13, 1919

Redlands.

It was sitting in the darkening ocean at the end of the dock.

Yesterday in Death Valley when Lloyd Garrison told us about Suzanne's post card, Mary remembered something from our visit to Montara. The name of Geller's Shipmaster.

Which was painted on the side of his yacht.

Redlands.

So it *wasn't* the name of some unknown town where Suzanne Smith had been staying when she worked at Gold Coast. It was Geller's yacht. She'd been living on her boss's yacht!

Once Mary had made the connection, we told Grayson about it, and he arranged for the Montara sheriff's office to go to Geller's estate and arrest Suzanne.

Naturally, the yacht was gone.

So was Geller.

So was his "assistant."

It was obvious that the bankrupt Geller and Suzanne Smith (his mistress?) had already sailed off to who-knows-where. So I immediately started contacting every harbormaster in the San Francisco area, but Geller's *Redlands* hadn't turned up at any of the SF marinas.

Then I tried a hunch.

I figured that a guy on the run like Geller, whom many believed was about to be indicted on fraud charges, would have taken his Shipmaster south toward balmy Mexico rather than north to chilly Canada in February.

So I decided to check out Santa Barbara, Los Angeles, San Diego, and all the other coastal towns in between, but I started with LA.

Starting with Marina del Ray.

The Marina Master called me back almost immediately.

Which he'd done earlier today, just before Kaplan called.

"The Redlands came in last night," he explained.

"Is it still there?"

"Yes."

Mary and I had to make a decision. Either go to meet with Kaplan or go to find Geller's yacht.

Well, you already know what happened at the Tar Pits, where we learned nothing new, and a man was dead.

With Kaplan lying dead at our feet, Mary looked up at me.

"We can't waste any time with the police right now, and there's nothing we can do for Kaplan. Let's head to the Marina, Billy, and you can call the police from a phone booth on the way."

Which I did.

Anonymously.

Now, as we were walking down the pier toward the *Redlands*, I stopped where I was, so Mary did the same.

I knew that I had to talk some sense into the world's most strongheaded woman.

"I need to board that yacht by myself," I told her. "We have no idea what might happen next."

She thought it over. Carefully. Yes, she was definitely headstrong, but she was never impetuous.

Or foolish.

She smiled.

"Are you planning to get the 'drop on them,' Billy?" she kidded, and I laughed.

"Exactly, just give me a few minutes, then you can board the yacht."

"Fine, I'll give you a few minutes."

I nodded and walked toward the Shipmaster, and Mary waited right where she was.

But I knew that she wouldn't stay there for very long.

It was now sunset over the ocean. It wasn't as dramatic as the Death Valley sundown we'd seen yesterday, but it was still quite marvelous.

Fortunately, I knew the marina pretty well because Fairbanks also kept his yacht anchored down here. He was friends with Moses Sherman, the famous developer who'd bought Port Ballona about fifteen years ago, then renamed it Playa Del Rey. In time, the marina had become the elite docks for the elite yachts of elite Angelinos. Especially, the Hollywood crowd, the politicians, and the entrepreneurs.

Not really my turf.

In truth, I'm not much of a boat guy. I've got nothing against them, but I'm a ranch guy who grew up in a saddle on the deserts of Arizona. I guess I'm more of a land animal.

I pulled my Colt and stepped onto the deck of the *Redlands*. The cabin door wasn't locked, so I opened it carefully and stepped inside. I went quietly down the stairs, passed the galley, then walked through the empty sitting/dining area. At the far end, I stepped into a spacious berth and saw Geller sitting on the far bunk staring up at me like an idiot. He was wearing white nautical clothes, and he looked like a silly child dressed up for a birthday party.

Suddenly, she was after me from nowhere.

In a frenzy.

I saw a knife, and I caught the crazed look in her eyes.

At first, that's all I saw.

The knife came down, and I stepped back to avoid it, but it slashed into my shoulder. Instinctively, I grabbed her wrist, but she fought back like the Furies. She was inordinately strong, and she kicked me, and she even tried to bite me. I felt that I had no choice. I smashed her on the side of her head with my Colt revolver, and she crumbled back into an empty bunk.

Unconscious.

I looked over at Geller, who seemed absolutely terrified.

"Is she dead?" he asked softly.

"Not at the moment," I said.

Then I took off my coat. My shirt was soaked with bright red blood, so I found a towel and pressed it into the wound.

It hurt like hell.

Yeah, I had an open wound in my shoulder, but much worse, I'd hit a woman. I didn't have much of a choice, but I still felt terrible about it.

Then Mary came down from the deck and immediately sized things up.

She was amazingly calm.

"Sit down, Billy, and take off your shirt."

I sat down on the bunk right next to the insensate Suzanne Smith.

Mary looked over at Geller, still sitting on the other bunk.

"First aid?"

When he pointed at one of the cabinets, Mary pulled out the kit and was soon tending to my injury. Doing her best to patch it up with gauze and tape.

"It's not as bad as it looks," I assured her.

It wasn't false bravado. The slice was long but not that deep, although I was fully aware that it would have been a whole lot deeper if I hadn't pulled back when Suzanne had first attacked me. She was uncannily strong, and in any other circumstance, I'm sure that her knife would have been buried to the hilt.

While Mary tended to me, Geller sat there like a moron.

I kept thinking of Humpty Dumpty.

At one point, I looked over at the little creep directly.

"If I hear *anything* that sounds like a lie, I'll go over there and break your neck then toss you into the ocean ten miles out."

Of course, I had no intention of doing any such

thing. For starters, I had absolutely no idea how to sail this huge contraption, but it certainly gave Mr. Geller something to think about while Mary finished patching up her cowboy/driver.

This time, there were no "drop on them" jokes.

Which I much appreciated.

When I was finally glued back together, I put my shirt back on, and Mary checked on Suzanne. She was still out like a light, but I knew that whenever she came back all hell would break loose, so I quickly bound her hands as well as her feet.

"Gag her, too," Mary said. "I don't want her disturbing my conversation with Mr. Geller."

"Gladly."

When Suzanne was properly gagged, Mary stepped closer to Geller and sat down facing him.

Very close.

I waited near the cabin doorway so I could keep an eye on Suzanne.

Mary looked at Geller.

"I expect the truth, Mr. Geller," she said firmly, "if I sense that you're not telling me the truth, I'll leave the boat and allow my associate do whatever he wishes."

Geller believed her.

He nodded.

"Good," she said. "Where were you planning to go in Mexico?"

"Puerto Vallarta," he shrugged. "Or maybe even Acapulco. Anywhere out of the US."

She seemed satisfied.

"Did you testify in court yesterday?"

"No, the trial was postponed until Monday."

Which was good to hear. Apparently, Martinez's

lawyer had managed to give us more time.

Now it seemed as though we were finally about to get to the heart of the matter:

What really happened on the day that David Durham was murdered.

But Mary threw a curve.

"What was Wendy Parker doing in LA?"

I wasn't sure what she was getting at, but Geller obviously understood.

"She was trying to figure out what happened to Durham," he explained.

"Why?"

He didn't hesitate.

"Because they were lovers."

Which really threw me for a loop.

"And she believed," Mary prompted, "that Charlene knew the truth about the murder?"

"Yes."

"Did you pay her way?"

He was clearly surprised that Mary had figured out his own involvement. So was I. But let's face it, not many receptionists can afford to stay at the Huntington Hotel in Pasadena.

"Yes, I helped her out."

"Why?"

"Because we had an agreement."

Mary didn't ask about the agreement; she just waited until Geller explained.

"I was also concerned about what had happened at Gold Coast that day, and to be honest, I felt like my life was in danger. I still do. That's why I'm heading to

Mexico. So I figured that if that foolish girl was planning to come down here to LA and snoop around, I wanted to know whatever she uncovered."

"So, you made an agreement?"

"Yes."

I couldn't restrain myself.

"Were you sleeping with her?" I butted in.

Mary didn't seem to mind.

"No."

He seemed to be telling the truth.

Mary pointed behind her at Suzanne lying on the bunk.

"What about that one? Were you sleeping with her?"

"Yes."

"Was she planning to go to Mexico with you?"

"Yes. Like me, she'd made a mess of things, and she just wanted to get away. So I agreed."

"How did she find you?"

"I guess Wendy must have told her. I'm not really sure, and I don't really care."

"Fine," Mary said, as if the "preliminaries" were over. "Now it's time to tell me *exactly* what happened that day at Gold Coast."

Geller shrugged again.

"It seems as if you already know."

"Then tell me what I already know."

I felt certain that Mary was bluffing, but Geller didn't seem to have a clue.

"When we were about to sign the contracts, David got cold feet and decided not to go ahead with the buyout."

"Why?"

"I'm not sure. I never got to ask him. But David was a lot tougher than I am, and I think he didn't like being bullied by Zukor's stooges. I don't know if it was a ploy to entice a larger offer, or if he just wanted to keep Gold Coast going. We were still making a pretty decent profit."

"Then what happened?"

"David told Kaplan that he'd reconsidered and that he was sorry that the man had made the trip to San Francisco for nothing. He was very polite about it. Then he nodded at everyone and left for his office. I never saw him again."

He corrected himself.

"Not alive."

The last bit clearly upset the little weasel, and I guess that he and Durham were not only business partners but friends as well.

Mary gave Geller a few moments to collect himself, then she pressed forward.

"And then?"

"Then Sloan stepped over to the table, signed Durham's name on the contracts, and left the room. A few minutes later, we heard the gunshot, and I knew instantly what had happened. So did Kaplan. So did the two young women. I was terrified, as if frozen, and I'm sure that the others were as well. Then Kaplan and I went down to David's office, and it was horrible. Sloan was standing over the desk, and David was sitting in his chair with a bullet hole in his forehead. He was still upright, and his eyes were dead, and there was a red stream of blood running down the front of his face. It was the most horrible thing I've ever seen, and all I've wanted to do ever since is run away from it. But then my finances bellied up, and everything got delayed."

"Did Paramount ever pay you for the buyout?"

"No, not yet anyway, but I want nothing to do with any of them, especially that ugly thug Aaron Sloan."

"Are you certain that he killed David Durham?"

"As certain as anything."

Then Geller went silent and thought things over. Eventually, he looked back at Mary and remembered the scene.

"It's haunted me day and night. David dead in his chair. The stream of blood. The smell of cigar smoke, gunpowder, and Narcisse Noir."

Mary seemed surprised.

"How would you recognize that scent?" she asked.

It was a good question.

Geller just shrugged a shrug.

"My ex-wife used the stuff."

Which made sense.

Then Suzanne came alive on the bunk.

She squirmed a bit and tried to sit up, trying to talk through her gag.

With little effect.

We all ignored her.

Mary finished up with a few more questions before we searched the place. Then Mary found something interesting in Suzanne's luggage, and I found the name of a small hotel on a scrap of paper in Geller's wallet.

"Sunside Lodging."

I was pretty sure that I knew who was staying at Sunside!

I looked over at Mary.

It was time to call Grayson again so he could lock Suzanne in the county jail.

30. El Matador

Thursday, February 13, 1919

I saw him coming through the darkness.

He was holding a revolver, but so was I.

I'd been waiting out there for most of the night. I was sitting on Mary's little bench in the same garden in Malibu where Philip Campbell had fallen dead nine nights ago, which eventually led to our involvement in the Gold Coast mess.

It was probably about 2:00 a.m., and Mary should have been asleep by now inside her hideaway cottage right behind me, but a light was still on inside, and I knew that she was up and waiting.

We both had the feeling that Sloan was coming for her tonight.

So I was sitting in the moonlight, thinking about pretty Wendy and about how she'd duped me and used me. She'd been in love with her boss at Gold Coast, and when he was murdered, she came to LA looking for Charlene to find out what really happened. I was just some dumb cowboy she'd spotted at the burial of Philip Campbell. Since it was obvious that Mary had taken an interest in Charlene, Wendy must have assumed that she could get some useful information out of me.

Mary's dumb driver.

Which meant that:

The night at Million Dollar Theatre was just a performance.

That the night at the abandoned *Intolerance* set was yet another performance.

But, of course, her kisses were her very best performances.

They sure duped the hell out of me.

But I wasn't sitting in the dark "mooning" about it. I was sitting in the dark asking myself how I could have been such a fool.

Such a sucker.

I was mad at myself, and I promised myself that it would never happen again, although I wasn't exactly sure how I could make sure that it never happened again.

Oh, well, I wasn't the first idiot duped by a pretty face.

Then I saw him coming.

Even in the dark it was clear that it was Sloan. The guy must have been pretty desperate to want to kill the most famous woman in the world, but I guess he felt that she was about to expose him.

Soon.

I stood up silently.

"Stop right there, Sloan!"

Sloan, as I should have anticipated, was not the kind of guy who stopped for anything, especially when the electric chair or a life stretch in San Quentin was at stake.

He raised his weapon to blow my head off.

According to all reports, Aaron Sloan was an exceptional cop and detective. Very good with a handgun. But I was from Arizona down near the border, and I was much better.

Besides, the guy had given me no choice.

I shot him twice, once in each thigh, before he had a chance to pull the trigger. He fell to ground, and I stepped over and kicked his semi-automatic into the nearby bushes. He'd fallen backwards into a flower bed, staring up at the moon and the stars.

As expected, I soon heard Mary approaching from behind me.

Concerned.

"Are you all right, Billy?"

"I'm fine, but he's not."

Mary nodded and knelt down over Sloan.

"They've found fingerprints on the gun that killed David Durham," she said.

"Well, they're not mine," he said dismissively.

"We also know that you forged his signature."

"So what? Big deal. Nobody cares."

Maybe he was right.

I got irritated.

I didn't like his attitude. His disrespect toward Mary.

"You also fired at Mary on Catalina," I said angrily, assuming that it was true, "and killed Kaplan at the tar pits."

He laughed in my face.

"I don't know what you're talking about, kid."

Now I was even more irritated.

"You won't be laughing when we find the rifle," I

said, which seemed to shut him up. Maybe he hadn't hidden the weapon as well as he should have.

He looked at Mary.

"I've got two bleeding holes in my thighs," he said.

I guess he was looking for sympathy.

But I was fed up.

I lifted my right foot and placed it on top of his left thigh and pressed down. He cried out in pain.

I liked the sound of it.

"That's enough of that, Billy," Mary said with a certain reluctance.

Then she took Sloan's face in her hand and made him look up at her directly.

"Is Zukor behind all of this?"

I was completely surprised by the question. Did Mary really think that her close friend, her father figure, was actually pulling the strings on everything that had happened?

Sloan looked at her coldly, sarcastically.

"Who?"

I moved closer.

"I'd like to step on him again, Mary."

I knew that she wouldn't allow it, but Mary was an actress, and she delayed her response for quite a long time in the darkness of the night. Sloan, of course, lying helpless on his back, tried not to show his concern, but he wasn't much of an actor.

"I suppose you shouldn't, Billy," she decided.

Then she stood up and went back to her cottage to call Detective Grayson.

We were keeping the man busy.

Maybe he could throw Sloan into a cage right next to Suzanne Smith.

31. LA County Jailhouse

Friday, February 14, 1919

It was going to be a very unusual Valentine's Day.

Fairbanks, who was coming back to town on Monday, had sent a massive flower arrangement to the Malibu cottage. It seemed like overkill to me, but it made Mary smile.

Maybe I was now a confirmed romance skeptic.

Thanks, Wendy.

So what would you expect the world-famous Mary Pickford to be doing on Valentine's Day?

Why not go to the county jailhouse?

Grayson had called early this morning.

"She'll only talk to you."

Which was interesting.

The "she," of course, was Suzanne Smith, and the "you," of course, was Mary.

I drove the Packard over to the county jailhouse, and Grayson was waiting for us.

"Why me?" Mary asked.

"I have no idea," he admitted, "but I appreciate your coming over."

He smiled oddly, then he looked at Mary.

"Happy Valentine's Day, by the way."

It was the first time I'd seen him smile. It seems that even smileless cops are more romantic than I am.

Mary smiled as well.

"You also, Detective!"

He led us down a long corridor of jail cells. I wondered if Sloan would be lurking in one, but he wasn't. Mostly there were scruffy drunks and life-ravaged losers. At the far end of the corridor, Grayson stopped at an isolated cell and opened it up.

Suzanne Smith was sitting in the far corner of the tiny jail cell on her bunk with her legs pulled up in front of her. She was wearing a grey smock, and she looked at us like a wounded animal.

Rabid.

She shot a cold look at Grayson.

"Go away!"

Grayson, who was obviously prepared for such an eventuality, said nothing and immediately left the cell.

Suzanne looked up at me.

I was the one she'd attacked with a knife. I was also the one who'd smashed her face, knocked her unconscious, bound her feet and her hands, then gagged her mouth.

But she didn't seem to be holding a grudge.

Mary cleared the air anyway.

"He stays," she said.

That was that.

"Fine," Suzanne agreed, still looking at me oddly. "Who is this boy to you?"

She was talking to Mary about someone who was the same age as she was, and I wondered how I'd be described.

Her driver?

Her assistant?

"He's my protector."

I liked that a lot, so did Suzanne Smith.

"I wish I had one."

There was a small chair in the small cell, and Mary pulled it closer to Suzanne's bunk and sat down.

I stood off in the corner.

I made a mental note to never end up in a jail cell. The place was tiny, dark, dirty, and claustrophobic.

But Suzanne didn't seem to mind at all. Now that Grayson was gone, she seemed oddly comfortable. She dropped her long legs over the side of the bunk, then she sat upright on the edge of the bed facing Mary.

Towering over her.

A bit too close for my money.

"What did you want to see me about?" Mary began.

Suzanne smiled.

It was a pretty smile, yet rather odd given the circumstances.

"Nothing. Nothing at all! I just thought it would be fun to see Mary Pickford again before they do whatever they intend to do with me."

It seemed as though, from Suzanne's point of view, everything was finally real. As if up until now, it had been some kind of game.

"Well, I should tell you a few things first, Suzanne," Mary explained.

Suzanne shrugged.

"Fine. Tell me whatever you want to tell me."

"I know that you strangled your cousin."

What!

Where did that come from?

Was Mary fishing?

As for Suzanne, there was no reaction.

None.

"You could have done it with your hands, of course," Mary continued, "but you used your jump rope. It came to me yesterday when I found it in your luggage on the *Redlands*. I remembered going through your athletic bag on the back porch of Charlene's cottage in Topanga Canyon. There were spikes, leg weights, and dumbbells, but no skip rope, so I had the cops examine the one I found on the yacht."

Which was rather amazing, even though it didn't really prove anything.

Not yet.

Mary clarified.

"They found blood on the rope, and your handprints on the wooden handles, and we both know whose blood it'll turn out to be."

Suzanne seemed unfazed. As if she'd already anticipated the worst and didn't care. Who knows, maybe she felt that she deserved whatever was coming. After all, she'd abandoned her boyfriend, abandoned her newborn, claimed that her child had been kidnapped, strangled her cousin, and then absconded with the Maternal Charities' funds.

Then she went partying on Catalina, while successfully seducing Bryan Geller and convincing him to betray Wendy Parker and take her to Mexico instead.

She'd been a busy girl.

Mary switched gears.

"You were quite an athlete, Suzanne."

She liked the topic.

"I sure was. Two years ago, I won the California girls' track championships, and I was the *only* girl on the team! No one believes that, but you can look it up. For a while, I was even more famous in Death Valley Junction than Mary Pickford!"

She enjoyed the memory.

"Then you got pregnant," Mary pointed out.

"Exactly! Which changed everything. People used to think I was a bit goofy even before that, but once it happened, I changed for good. I really didn't care what happened next."

"Why?"

"I don't know."

It seemed as if she really didn't know.

Mary shifted gears again.

"Do you know who killed David Durham that day at Gold Coast?"

Suzanne just shrugged.

"I always thought it was Charlene."

"But wasn't she in the room with you and Geller and the others when the gunshot went off?"

Suzanne shook her head.

"I really don't remember. It's very confusing. I thought that Charlene had left the room before the gunshot went off, but maybe I'm wrong. I've been confused about a lot of things for a long time now. Long before Lloyd got me pregnant."

"At the time of the murder, you were Geller's assistant, correct?"

She found it amusing and laughed.

"Yes, and I was the dumbest assistant in the history of dumb assistants."

"Were you sleeping with him?"

"Of course, I was! He had lots of money and a big, beautiful boat, and he went nuts over me. Why wouldn't he?"

She seemed proud of herself.

"Then what happened?"

"Just like we planned, I came down here to have the baby in LA, but Bryan got into some serious money trouble, and he stopped taking my calls. I also think that he was totally spooked by Durham's murder, so once again I was suddenly on my own."

"So you dumped the baby at Charlene's in Topanga Canyon and told the police that someone had kidnapped your child."

"Yes, it seemed pretty clever at the time, but then I got worried that Charlene would tell the police the truth."

"Did she threaten you about it?"

"Yeah, but I wouldn't call it a threat. Charlene was much too sweet for that, but she did tell me that I'd have to come clean sooner or later."

"Then her father was killed, so you killed Charlene so that no one would know the truth."

"Yes, but I did it quickly, Miss Pickford. She didn't suffer much. To be honest, I'd always liked her."

"Then you left her dead in the bed, with your baby asleep in the other bed."

"Yes. I knew that somebody would take care of the baby, and they did, and I assume that Lloyd's got it now. Well, good for him."

I'm almost ashamed to admit it, but it was extremely interesting being in a small confined space with such a deranged yet rather articulate human being. I'd known a few weirdos in the army and on the rodeo circuit, but nothing like this.

This was beyond weird.

It was also creepy as hell.

Mary, however, seemed unfazed.

At least, on the surface.

She still wasn't finished.

"Did you kill Philip Campbell?"

"No, I liked Philip a lot, and I wasn't even there when he died."

"Do you know who did it?"

"I've got no idea, Miss Pickford. Maybe those Zukor people, especially that big scary guy."

Having spent some time with both Sloan and Suzanne, I can guarantee you that Suzanne was much scarier.

Mary thought things over.

The whole mess.

"Do you realize what will happen to you, Suzanne?"

She shrugged a second time.

"Yeah, they probably won't zap me because I'm a woman, and they'll also figure out that I'm more than a bit nuts. So they'll send me off to some women's prison. So what? Big deal! I can handle it. I can handle anything."

I had the feeling that she was right about that.

I had the feeling that she'd soon be jumping rope in her prison cell (if they'll let her have a rope), and that all the other inmates would be terrified of her.

"Maybe you can handle it, Suzanne, but you need to find some peace within yourself, some peace with God, some peace with what you've done."

"Hell, Miss Pickford, I'm already at peace!"

She seemed eerily convincing.

[Yes, it's very strange, Billy, but I often think of her and wonder what's going on in her disordered mind. If she's ever truly realized what she's done. Whenever I think of her, I find myself praying for her.]

Later, Grayson led us out of her dungeon into the light.

Into the California sun.

It felt wonderful.

Maybe it could burn away the ickiness.

"Did you find the rifle?" Mary asked the detective when we were finally alone and could speak privately.

"Yes," Garrison assured her, "and the cartridges too. We found it in his apartment closet. I guess that Sloan felt he was invulnerable. I think he believed that Paramount would never mess with him because he 'knows stuff.' Whatever the case, it was pretty stupid."

"What was it?" I wondered.

"A Winchester 1910."

I knew it well.

It was surely the rifle that had fired at Mary on Catalina and had also killed Howard Kaplan at the La Brea Tar Pits. Who knows what else it's done.

"There's more good news," Grayson continued. "We found a witness, two witnesses in fact, who saw Sloan that evening at the tar pits. He was carrying a rifle, quickly got into his sedan, and drove away."

Grayson looked directly at Mary.

"We've got him, Miss Pickford! He's finished!"

The detective smiled once again.

He was having quite a Valentine's Day.

32. Death Valley Junction

Friday, February 14, 1919

We were back in the furnace again.

It had been another long drive across the state into the heats of the Mojave directly to the front door of Mrs. Bedford's little white house.

She opened the door like a condemned woman.

Once again, Mary and the wary woman sat on the couch, as I melted into the same living room chair as the last time.

The gun rack was no longer empty.

There was no talk of lemonade.

Mary got right to it.

"The police will be coming soon, Mrs. Bedford."

She knew.

"I know."

Mary gestured to the gun rack.

"Is that the rifle?"

"Yes."

Meaning the Springfield '80 that Philip Campbell had told us had shot him twice in the back before he died in Mary's garden in Malibu.

"I understand it's a rather rare rifle."

"I believe it is," Mrs. Bedford agreed. "It was once my husband's."

"I should also tell you that you've been identified by a hotel clerk at Beverly Bungalows where you stayed during your trip to LA."

That was Grayson's work. Mary and I weren't the only ones trying to unravel all the murders.

Mrs. Bedford was clearly resigned, but she did make an effort to explain herself.

"I didn't intend to kill him."

"What happened?" Mary asked.

The answer seemed like a non-sequitur.

"It's lonely out here in the desert, Miss Pickford."

Which was easy to believe.

Her husband had died a few years ago, and she was still an attractive widow, only thirty-four years old, and living alone in the middle of nowhere.

We waited for more.

"It was horrible after my husband died, but then Philip Campbell took an interest. He was perfectly marvelous, and we became happy lovers. We even talked about marriage."

She stopped, lost deep in her past, lost in all her might-have-beens.

"Then Charlene took an interest in acting," Mary prompted.

"Yes, and I have to admit she was pretty good at it. In the church plays. In the high school plays. Then she got it into her young girl's head to go to Hollywood."

"But they went to San Francisco first."

"Yes, because Philip knew someone at Gold Coast Distributors, and they felt that any kind of job in the business would be a good start before they went down to LA.”

The widow looked directly at Mary.

“I certainly don’t begrudge a young girl having her dreams, but she was seventeen years old, and she could take care of herself. Why did Philip have to go with her?”

It was the unanswered question of her life.

“What did he tell you?”

“That he didn’t love me anymore.”

She said it as if she couldn’t believe that she was actually saying it out loud.

That it was an undeniable fact.

“Sure,” she continued, “at first, he told me that he was just going along with Charlene to help her get settled. That he’d be returning soon. Which still made me nervous and wary, so I begged him not to leave, but he wouldn’t change his mind, then he and his daughter took off for San Francisco.”

“How’d you track him to LA?”

“There was an obnoxious receptionist sitting at the front desk in the empty Gold Coast building, and when I told her I was a family friend of the Campbells, she was dismissive and disrespectful. So I went out to my car and took out the old Springfield. I’d really only brought it along for protection in the big city. After all, I’m a desert girl. But now I was angry, so I went back inside and pointed the barrel at the stupid receptionist. Right in her stupid face, and she got scared as hell, and she told me what I wanted to know.”

“Where did you meet with Philip?”

“We met one night at a tiny Mexican restaurant near Zuma Beach. As odd as it seems now, we had a very pleasant dinner together. Delicious enchiladas and

Sangria. Philip was especially thoughtful and kind that night, but he was also firm. He was committed to staying in LA to help out his daughter. He even mentioned that Charlene had met you somewhere, and that you'd offered to help her out. Naturally, I tried to talk him out of it, and I kept insisting. Getting more and more emotional. More and more frustrated. Finally, he gently took my hands into his, looked deep into my eyes, and told me that he didn't love me anymore. I was absolutely stunned. Disbelieving. Devastated."

She still was.

Then Mary took her hands into her own.

"Then you shot him, Irene?" she asked softly.

"Yes, dear, I did. We went outside into the little parking lot. It was very late, and there was no one around, and I felt as if I was losing my mind. As if my life was coming to an end. When Philip said, 'Goodnight, Irene, take care of yourself,' I removed the Springfield from the back of my car, and I shot him twice in the back as he walked away. I did it without the slightest sense of anger. I did it unthinkingly. I did it as naturally as I might have waved goodbye to the one I loved. Then I immediately pushed it from my mind, and I drove off into the darkness heading for the desert."

"Do you know why he drove to my house that night?"

"I have no idea, but maybe he thought that I would go after Charlene, and that he wouldn't make it back to Topanga Canyon in time. So maybe he thought that you would call for help. That you would send someone to protect Charlene. I don't really know. The whole thing still seems like a dream. Like a nightmare."

Which logistically made some sense. Zuma's only a few miles drive from El Matador, even for an almost dead man.

At this point, there didn't seem to be anything else to discuss.

Mrs. Bedford dabbed at her eyes a bit then stood up from the couch.

She looked at Mary.

"I'd better change before they take me away."

When she left the room, Mary looked over at me.

"I don't like it, Billy."

Which I assumed meant I should get up and keep an eye on Mrs. Bedford. Which seemed odd to me since Mrs. Bedford surely wasn't about to make a break for the back door and try to escape across the Mojave Desert.

Besides, the woman said she was going to change her clothes, and I certainly didn't want to barge into her bedroom and see any of that.

Nevertheless, I did what Mary wanted.

I stood up and walked through the thick heats of the house to the bedroom door. It dawned on me that maybe Mary was afraid that Mrs. Bedford might have another weapon in her bedroom and that she might try to kill the both of us before the police arrived.

Which I know sounds ridiculous, but let's face it, she'd already killed a man at Zuma Beach.

I knocked on her door.

No response.

"I'm coming in, Mrs. Bedford."

When there was still no response, I opened the door.

Mrs. Bedford was taking something from a shelf

high in her closet with her back to me.

"Do you need some help with something?" I offered stupidly.

She turned around.

She had a gun in her hand.

A semi-automatic.

Probably a Beretta of some kind.

As for me, I still had nothing in my hands, even though my Colt was in my shoulder holster.

She looked at me oddly.

Determined.

Fortunately, it wasn't my head that she was planning to blow apart.

She immediately pressed the barrel under her chin, aiming the barrel up through her head toward her brain.

"Please, just leave me alone, young man."

She was very polite about it.

I had no idea what to do.

I was only a few steps away.

"You still have the safety on," I tried.

She believed me and lowered the gun to check.

I dove at her and drove the two of us into the bottom of the closet. It wasn't my slickest move, but the Beretta went flying.

It was all over.

I stood up and helped Mrs. Bedford to her feet as Mary entered the room.

Mary bent down and picked up the gun.

I guess she was worried about suicide when she sent me into the bedroom.

Defeated, Mrs. Bedford looked over at Mary and apologized.

"I thought it was for the best," she said.

It was terribly sad.

Fortunately, the local cops arrived soon afterward, and Mary and I got the hell out of there, eager for the long drive back to LA.

33. Kinney Pier

Saturday, February 15, 1919

I walked out on Kinney Pier.

It was late morning, and the sky above was blue and cloudless over the deep Pacific.

There was a slight breeze in the air, which I much appreciated after the heavy heats of the desert yesterday.

I've always liked Venice Beach.

It seemed too weird not to like.

Am I right?

Here we are on the far Pacific coast, six thousand miles from Venice, Italy, where some guy decided about fifteen years ago to create a little resort town with canals, gondolas, and an arcaded street with Italian architecture.

And that wasn't all.

The same guy (a developer named Abbot Kinney) also built a pier, which he named after himself, with an auditorium, a restaurant shaped like a ship, a dance hall, and lots of gaming booths and amusement rides.

I strolled past the Aquarium, then the miniature railroad, the Racing Derby, the Whip, and the Virginia

Reel, heading toward the end of the pier.

She was waiting at the railing, staring at the endless ocean.

I came up behind her.

"Miss Addison?" I said softly.

She turned around.

She was very pretty.

Very.

She looked a bit like Coleen Moore, but younger.

Arlene Addison had shortish dark hair, dark brown eyes, and a smile that I liked more than a lot. She was dressed in a lovely white sweater and a white skirt, and she had a small white flower in her hair.

I'm not very smart about flowers, but I think it was probably a peony of some kind.

"Yes," she said.

"I appreciate your coming."

"You said on the phone that it had something to do with Mary Pickford, so here I am."

I didn't want to mislead her, so I got right to the point.

"It really has more to do with Owen Moore."

She seemed surprised, even confused.

"Owen Moore?"

"Yes, and please forgive me for being so blunt, but Miss Pickford's been told that you've had some kind of relationship with her husband."

"What? Absolutely not! Never!"

She looked at me with a little blaze in her dark brown eyes.

She was very convincing, and she was also insulted.

"Besides," she continued, "there's blunt, and then there's blunt! Just who are you anyway?"

"As I said on the phone, I work for Miss Pickford. My name is Billy Kidd."

She smiled at my name.

I get that a lot.

"Are you another one of those fake Hollywood cowboys?"

Now *I* was insulted.

"I'm the real deal, young lady. Direct from my father's ranch in Tucson, Arizona."

"I see," she said with a mischievous smile, "I guess you haven't learned your proper manners yet."

I liked her.

Let's face it, she'd been good enough to meet with me, and then I'd immediately started casting aspersions.

"Are you an actress?" I tried.

"Who isn't in this town? I'm just a girl from Encino trying to do my best."

"Any work?"

"A few bits at Universal. Not much."

"Did you ever meet Owen Moore?"

"Yes, once at Universal, and we had lunch afterward with a bunch of other people. That was it, Mr. Billy the Kidd. I never saw him again. So, what's this all about anyway?"

I figured I should be honest.

"Moore is claiming that you're blackmailing him."

Her shock was mixed with amusement.

"Blackmailing him! How?"

"He says that you had an affair, that he sent you some letters of promise, and that now you're threatening to release them to the press unless he pays you off."

"That's completely absurd! There was *no* affair, and there were *no* letters. To be honest, I didn't even like the guy. He was an Irish blowhard, and he stunk of whiskey in the afternoon, and I remember feeling sorry for Mary Pickford. How did she end up with such a loser?"

"She married him way too young."

It was the best I could offer.

Arlene seemed to understand.

"Young women often make blunders," she said thoughtfully.

"Including young women from Encino?" I kidded.

"No chance, cowboy! My mommy put me on guard at an early age."

"Good girl. Keep it up."

She smiled again.

"Having said that," I continued, "how about I take you to lunch with no strings attached?"

She thought it over, then looked at me directly.

"Will you behave yourself, Billy Kidd?"

"I always do, Arlene, even if my manners are a bit raw."

She liked my answer, but she was still hesitant, so I tried another tack.

"You don't realize it, Arlene, but you've done Miss Pickford an invaluable service today, and I'm very grateful, and she will be as well. Let me tell you about it over lunch."

She laughed.

It was a lovely laugh.

"Well, how could I say no to that?"

34. Sunside Lodging

Saturday, February 15, 1919

The place was a dump.

Sunset Lodging on Figueroa.

I'd looked it over when I first got to town, and I decided that it was even too tawdry for an injured down-and-out cowboy.

It was a far cry from the Huntington.

I knocked on the front door and stared at the peeling blue paint.

Wendy opened the door.

She was astonished to see me and not too happy about it.

But I have to admit, she looked quite marvelous.

Even in her third-rate dump.

She wore a light-yellow jacket over a light-yellow blouse above a light-yellow skirt. As always, her long blonde hair was thick and long and ever flowing, and her eyes were bright blue against all that yellow.

She said nothing.

"Can I come in?" I suggested.

She thought it over.

"Well," I warned her, "I'm coming in anyway."

She relented and held the door open. The small darkish room had a tiny cot, an upright chair, a small closet, and four blank walls. I figured that the bathroom was somewhere outside and down the corridor. Shared with some of the other guests. The smell in her room was an odd mixture of Wendy's perfume and Sunside mildew.

Wendy sat back on the neatly made cot. There was a novel lying on the bed next to her.

A romance.

Naturally.

"What do you want, Billy?" she asked impatiently.

"Maybe a little bit of the truth."

"What does that mean?"

"It means that I know that you were working with Geller until he flipped you over for Suzanne Smith."

"Well, she's much more inclined to spread her legs than I am."

Which seemed accurate enough, although remarkably crude.

"Well, I won't ask what *you* did with David Durham."

"Then don't, Billy! It's none of your business."

Maybe it wasn't.

She calmed herself down, then she got friendly.

She looked at me seductively.

"You know I really did care for you, Billy, but my life was too much of a mess."

"You used me to get information about whatever Mary and I knew about the Campbells."

She made no effort to deny it.

"Yes, that was my motive in the beginning."

"Did you do the same thing with Royce Reynolds?"

Meaning the bit actor who was hanging around Charlene Campbell at her father's burial.

Wendy shrugged.

"No, I didn't. But I did pay that colossal idiot to get close to Charlene, but he proved to be useless. There was never anything to it. Never anything intimate. I was just trying to find out what had happened to David. Trying to find out who had killed him at Gold Coast, and I'd convinced Geller to pay my expenses. So, yes, I used Geller, and I used Reynolds, and I used you. At first. But then I started falling for you, Billy, and it got very confusing. David had been killed just a few months earlier, and now I was forgetting all about him, and I was angry with myself, so I cut you off."

I believed some of it, but certainly not all of it.

"I really did have feelings for you, Billy, and I still do."

I didn't buy it, so I changed the subject.

"Why are you still in LA?"

She shrugged again.

"Because I've got nowhere else to go. I've run out of money. Geller's been taken back to San Francisco to be indicted on fraud charges, and the *Redlands* has been impounded by the courts. On Monday, I'm planning to look for work somewhere so I can make enough money to get back to San Francisco and start over."

"Why didn't you ask me for help?"

"Why do you think, Billy? I was too ashamed. I felt that I'd already burned down that bridge."

She certainly had.

There was a knock at the door.

One that I was expecting.

Once again, Wendy looked totally astonished.

She looked over at me.

"Do you know who that is?"

I said nothing, stood up, and opened the door.

Detective Grayson stepped inside, followed by a rather famous actress.

Wendy clearly didn't like what she was seeing, but I couldn't tell if she realized that the jig was finally up.

Probably not.

She probably figured that she could still wiggle her way out of anything.

I moved the room's only chair closer to the cot, and Mary sat down so she could face Wendy directly. Grayson, like me, stood back against the front wall. I guess he felt that Mary could get more information out of the lying receptionist than he could.

"I wonder if we could talk a bit, Wendy," Mary said, "before Detective Grayson arrests you."

Wendy seemed unconcerned, still confident.

"I like your pictures very much, Miss Pickford."

"Thank you, Wendy."

Which was followed by a long silence in the little room.

It was time for Mary to blow things up.

"Detective Grayson now has the Smith & Wesson that you used to kill David Durham, and your fingerprints have been positively identified on the weapon."

What?

Whose fingerprints?

I thought that Grayson was just picking up Wendy for some questioning about Sloan. Was Mary bluffing? Did Wendy actually murder the man she loved?

It seemed that she did from the look on her face.

She was trapped, and she knew it.

I now realized that Wendy hadn't come down to LA to find out what had happened when her lover was killed. She'd come to LA to secure the incriminating murder weapon.

Using everyone in her path.

Including me.

"There's no doubt about it, Wendy, so you might as well tell me the truth."

Mary was gentle, and Wendy thought it over.

To be honest, I had no idea what was coming next.

Then Wendy looked directly at Mary and explained.

"He threw me over, Miss Pickford. I slept with the man for a month, and he promised to take me to Paris after the buyout."

"Then he decided against the buyout," Mary prompted.

"Yes, and he decided against me as well."

She had tears in her eyes.

Not gushing, but real tears, not fake ones.

Tears, of course, for herself.

Mary passed her a handkerchief.

Wendy dabbed lightly at her eyes then continued softly.

"He sat behind his desk, and he told me that it was over. No buy out. No Paris. Nor more 'us.' He was finished with me. David had used me like a silly fool, and I went out of my mind."

"Tell me."

"I knew that he kept a gun in his file cabinet, so I opened it up, took it out, and shot him in the forehead. I didn't even think about it. It just happened. As if it wasn't me doing what I'd actually just done. At first, I didn't even realize what had happened, but when I saw the blood streaming down his face, I dropped the gun on his desk, left the office, and returned to my chair at the reception desk. As if nothing had happened. I must have been in shock. In denial. It wasn't until later when I saw Zukor's thug going into the office that I realized what I'd done, and that I'd surely end up in jail for the rest of my life. But then Zukor's men conveniently dumped the blame on Carlos Martinez, and the murder weapon was supposedly missing. Surely, it had been taken by that big guy Sloan."

"So you assumed that you'd gotten away with it."

"It seemed as though I had, and I tried to push it from my mind. Then two months later, when I was helping Geller shut down Gold Coast for Paramount, I was sitting at my desk and Sloan walked into the building. He came up to my desk, towered above me, and I was terrified."

"What did he want?"

"He wanted the gun. He leaned over my desk and wrapped his right hand around my neck and said, 'Where's Charlene Campbell?' All I could do was shake my head to let him know that I had no idea, which wasn't the truth, but he believed me."

"Which made you realized that he'd never had the gun in the first place."

"Exactly."

"Which made you start thinking that maybe Charlene had taken it."

"That's correct."

"Why did Sloan want the gun?"

"He said that he no longer trusted Zukor's lawyer Kaplan, who was convinced that he'd killed David. So he wanted the weapon just in case any accusations were ever made against him."

"To protect himself?"

"Yes, for leverage."

"So, it sounds like Sloan believed that Charlene had killed David Durham."

"Yes, after the gunshot, he'd seen her coming out of David's office then leaving through the back exit. This was after I'd returned to my desk. But Sloan couldn't find her in San Francisco since she was living under a false name in LA."

"So you decided that you needed to get the gun from Charlene."

"Yes, for obvious reasons."

Meaning the fingerprints.

"Why do you think that Charlene took the gun?"

"I have no idea, maybe she thought that her wacko cousin had killed David, and she wanted to protect her."

"Or maybe," Mary speculated, "she'd unthinkingly picked up the gun and was afraid that she'd be suspected of the murder."

"Maybe."

"Then you made your deal with Geller."

"Yes, by then the little jerk was running scared, and he was very easy to manipulate. His finances had taken a serious tumble, he was being investigated for investment fraud, and he was still terrified of Zukor's men. He believed that Sloan had killed David, so I told him that I would go to LA and get the murder weapon from Charlene, which would give both of us leverage and protection from Zukor. So Geller agreed to finance my trip, but Charlene told me that her father had already 'taken care' of the gun and that he'd never hand it over to me. Regardless, I wasn't about to give up, but then both Philip and Charlene were murdered within a few days of each other."

"Then you went back to San Francisco."

"Yes, twice. I didn't want to, but Geller needed me to shut down Gold Coast for Zukor. At that point, I was the only employee left, and Geller wanted me to handle everything. The guy was afraid of his own shadow, and he never even returned to his own office. He just hid out at his bankrupt estate in Montara making plans to sail the *Redlands* down to Mexico."

"Wasn't he planning to go with Suzanne Smith?"

Wendy laughed.

"Yes, at first. They'd been sleeping together ever since she'd arrived in San Francisco. He hired her as his secretary, and I think they slept together her first night on the job. Suzanne wasn't one to waste time, and she kept the moron on the hook even after she told him that she was pregnant by her old boyfriend back in Death Valley. Naturally, Geller got spooked about that, so she told him that she was giving the baby to Charlene."

"Which was a lie."

"Which was a lie. A typical Suzanne lie. Charlene, of course, knew nothing about it until she came home one day and found a newborn baby sleeping on her couch in Topanga Canyon."

"How did Suzanne find her in LA?"

Wendy shook her head and scoffed.

"Exactly the same way I did. Charlene confided in

both of us about the name changes and about where she was staying in LA with her father. Charlene was a sweetheart, but very naïve and not nearly as cautious as her father wanted her to be. In the end, it got her killed."

Mary thought things over, then backtracked a bit.

"So you convinced Geller to betray Suzanne and take you to Mexico instead?"

"Which was easy to do. Suzanne's a lot of fun, but she's nutty as the day is long. She's also a loose cannon. In truth, she's loose about everything. Geller got spooked, and he did exactly what I told him to do."

Then Wendy looked over at me.

"Geller and I were never lovers, Billy, but we had a mutual interest in getting away from everything."

Unimpressed, I said nothing.

Mary, of course, didn't want Wendy to get distracted.

"Then Suzanne turned the tables on you, right?"

Wendy laughed at the irony.

"Yeah, she knew that Geller was planning to dock the *Redlands* in Marina del Rey, so she went down there, took her clothes off, and I was suddenly out of the picture."

Wendy looked around the small barren room.

"I ended up living in this dump with no prospects. A far cry from Paris. Maybe jail won't be so bad after all."

"Dump" was exactly the right word.

Wendy looked over at Grayson.

"Anything else?" she asked.

He definitely had another loose end to tie up.

"Did you send that anonymous note to Adolph

Zukor intended for Mary. The one that said, 'Destroy it or else'?"

"Yes, I knew that Philip had left everything to Miss Pickford, which I assumed included the murder weapon, so I thought that maybe I could scare Miss Pickford into getting rid of it."

She looked at Mary.

"Obviously, you don't scare very easily."

Wendy looked back at Grayson.

"Is that it?"

"For now."

"Will the fact that I was out of my mind when I pulled the trigger help me in the courtroom?"

"That's for a jury to decide."

"What do *you* think?"

Grayson shrugged.

"I think it might keep you out of the chair."

Meaning the electric chair.

It wasn't very encouraging.

Grayson walked over to the cot.

"Please stand up, Miss Parker, and turn around."

Wendy did, and he cuffed her wrists.

It was the second time in two days that Mary and I had watched as a jilted woman was handcuffed for murder.

Did I feel sorry for Wendy?

Yes, I did. A bit.

Mary once said, "It's not easy to be a woman, Billy," and I'm sure that she's right.

Before Grayson and his prisoner exited the dump, Wendy looked back at me.

"I really did like you, Billy."

I said nothing.

Then they were gone.
Mary looked over at me.
"I believe her, Billy. Don't you?"
"A bit."

35. Busch Gardens

Monday, February 17, 1919

Mary was back in her element!

Acting.

She was sitting on the rocks over a small pond in Busch Gardens.

Next to Mahlon Hamilton.

It was a scene from *Daddy-Long-Legs*, and Hamilton was playing her love interest Jarvis Pendleton.

As for me, I was standing alone behind the camera and the crew. Enjoying myself. Enjoying Mary's obvious enjoyment. Enjoying the beautiful California afternoon. Enjoying the fact that all the dangers had passed, and that all the murders had been resolved.

Enjoying lovely Busch Gardens.

Mary had told me earlier that they'd once been the personal gardens of Adolphus Busch (the beer guy) before he opened it to the public over a decade ago. The place was magnificent. Full of colorful flowers, striking statuary, and peaceful ponds.

Even waterfalls.

Now a film crew.

Mary told me a while back that she'd become hooked on acting when she was a little girl performing on the Toronto stage. Later, when she desperately needed money for the family, she reluctantly decided to "demean" herself by working in films. Later, after making many short films with DW Griffith, she got another opportunity to appear on Broadway in another Belasco play. Something called *A Good Little Devil*. But it wasn't the same. Mary discovered, to her astonishment, that she missed films too much, so instead she signed a contract to make more films with Adolph Zukor.

As Mary had once told *Photoplay*, "Whenever I stand in front of a camera, it's just like heaven."

Well, she was now back in "heaven" after the Influenza had knocked her out of action for a while. All was right in Mary's world. Doug Fairbanks was back in town, and her mother was returning on the evening train.

Earlier, on the drive to Pasadena, I told her about Arlene Addison. I didn't know if she'd be displeased that I'd gone behind her back, or if she'd appreciate my initiative.

As well as the outcome.

"I met with Owen's supposed mistress," I started.

Mary was surprised.

"How do you know she's the right one?"

"Spector told me."

She was suspicious.

"And what does he want in return?"

"Just some heads-up on whatever you're working on next. I hope that's OK."

"It's fine, Billy."

We both knew that such secrets are never kept secret for very long. Sooner or later, some reporter always figures out what's happening next and gets the "scoop," so what difference did it make if it was Maurice Spector?

"Don't worry," I assured her, "I'll check with you before I tell him anything."

"I know you will, Billy. Who is she?"

"A bit actress from Encino. She's been in a few of Tom Mix's pictures. She says that there was never an affair, never any letters, and never any blackmail."

"You believe her?"

"I do. Apparently, she only met him once."

Mary got suspicious again.

"Is she pretty?"

I laughed.

"All actresses are pretty."

Mary laughed as well.

"Have you asked her out yet?"

"Not yet, after all, my recent track record's pretty lousy."

"Don't blame yourself, Billy. Wendy duped a lot of people."

Yeah, that was nothing but the truth.

"Regardless," I said, "your husband's definitely lying."

I didn't use the word extortion.

Mary thought it over.

"It's certainly not the first time," she said sadly.

Then she looked over at me directly, which I could "sense" even though I was driving the car and keeping my eyes on the road ahead.

"I appreciate it, Billy. I really do."

I believed her, even though, of course, I wasn't sure if it would make any difference. Would she confront him about his deception? Would she refuse his next attempt to weasel money out of her?

I had no idea.

That was between the wife and her husband.

I could feel her smile in the seat next to me.

"Somebody's becoming quite the detective!" she kidded.

"Look who's talking!" I kidded right back.

When the poignant scene on the rocks was finished, the set shut down. Mary spent some time talking things over with her director Mickey Neilan and her photographer Charles Rosher. When it seemed that they'd fully prepared for tomorrow's shoot, she walked over to her driver.

Me.

"How's my detective?" she said with a smile.

"Enjoying himself!"

Then a black Rolls-Royce Silver Ghost pulled up on Crags Road.

Zukor's car.

The boss got out, walked over to Mary, and nodded at me.

It wasn't a "leave us alone" nod, so I stayed right where I was.

He looked down at Mary.

"How's my honey?"

"Happy to be back in action."

It was clear how much they cared for each other, even though they weren't working together anymore, and I was glad that we'd never found any evidence implicating Zukor in what had happened at Gold Coast or in any kind of coverup after the fact.

It seemed that he'd been oblivious to what really happened.

He looked over at the mostly abandoned set.

"How's Mickey behaving?" he asked.

"Mostly sober."

"Excellent."

Then he looked at her directly.

"I'm sorry about Sloan, Mary. I knew he was a tough guy and that's why I hired him, but I had no idea that he was the kind of man he was."

Which irritated me a bit, so I butted in where I shouldn't have butted in.

"A murderer, you mean. And a man who fired a rifle at Miss Pickford."

I waited to see how the man who ran Paramount would respond to the accusations of a man who drove a Packard for a living.

He looked at me directly.

"You're absolutely right, young man. It seems that I put Mary in danger, and I'm glad that you were always with her. To help her and protect her."

I just nodded, grateful that whoever was replacing Sloan wouldn't be trapping me in an alley later tonight.

"Enough of that," Mary said, "let's just be grateful that everything's worked out all right."

"Yes," Z agreed, "and I must admit I was shocked to hear that the receptionist did it."

But I still wasn't finished making a nuisance of myself.

"Yes," I said, "and Mary knew before anyone else."

Z looked at Mary.

"Even before the fingerprints were verified?"

"Yes," she admitted.

Zukor was astonished.

"How?"

"The perfume."

Narcisse Noir.

Which I'd learned is a very unique fragrance created by the House of Caron, which highlights both Narcissus and African Orange. I thought it was just some sweet scent that made Wendy irresistible.

Mary explained to Zukor with a smile.

"I first smelled it off my Billy Boy after he'd been on a date with her one night. Then I smelled it again when we talked to her at Gold Coast. Then the next day, when we went to Montara to talk to Geller, he said that he'd smelled the same perfume in Durham's office right after the murder."

"How did Geller recognize it?" Zukor wondered.

"His ex-wife used it."

The movie boss shook his head in amazement.

"You're a ridiculous marvel, Miss Mary!"

At that point, I decided that I should give them some privacy, so I nodded at both of them, then walked over to Mary's Packard.

Thinking how blessed I was!

Working for the most famous woman in the world!

Working for one of the kindest women in the world!

Working in the midst of fascinating Hollywood!

Working on narrative writing strategies with Mary Pickford and Francis Marion!

And still only eighteen years old!

Maybe if my writing gets good enough someday, I'll tell the story of how an actress and a young cowboy solved the terrible murder of Philip Campbell.

And Charlene Campbell.

And Howard Kaplan.

And David Durham.

Maybe someday.

Let's see what happens.

Then off in the distance, Adolph Zukor kissed Miss Mary goodbye on the top of her head, and she turned around and started walking toward me and her Packard.

I held the door open.

Happily.

[My dearest Billy, I loved reading the manuscript and enjoyed all the memories, but I do wonder if you should publish it. Is it too self-serving? Will the reader think I'm too inflated? After all, you did as much as I did. Anyway, think it over. I'll support, of course, whatever you decide to do. With many lovings, your Mary.]

Editors' Note:

After his death in 1958, the present manuscript was found in the papers of William Kidd, the noted author of *Arizona Sundown* and numerous other best-selling western novels. It seems to have been written in 1933. Also found in 1958 was a copy of a short handwritten note that Mr. Kidd sent to Mary Pickford along with a copy of the original manuscript. The note was dated August 29, 1933:

> My Dearest Mary,
> Enclosed is the manuscript we discussed on the phone last year. Please let me know what you think, and please feel free to mark it up! I hope that all continues to go well in your life. As for me, I'm perfectly content back here in Arizona scribbling away on the family ranch!
> I'll write again soon at much greater length.
> God bless, Miss Mary!
> Always, your Billy

Mary's few comments were written in red on the manuscript (bracketed in the text) which was returned to Mr. Kidd. Whether there was a more extensive response is unknown. For whatever reason, William Kidd decided not to publish the manuscript at the time, but last year his daughter and literary heir, Mary Pickford Kidd, decided to do so after the passing of Miss Pickford. It was also decided by Mary Kidd and the editors to include Mary Pickford's few short comments in brackets within the book, as well as the responsorial additions that William made within the manuscript, which were handwritten on the backs of the relevant pages.

We remain extremely grateful to the entire Kidd family for their permission to publish this most curious and revealing memoir.

William Baer is the award-winning author of more than thirty books including the Jack Colt mystery series *New Jersey Noir*, the Deirdre Flanagan mystery series, *Companion, Advocatus Diaboli, Times Square and Other Stories, Classic American Films*, and *One-and-Twenty Tales*. A graduate of Rutgers, NYU, South Carolina, the Johns Hopkins Writing Seminars, and USC Cinema, he's been the recipient of a Guggenheim Fellowship, a Fulbright (Portugal), an NEA fellowship in fiction, and the Jack Nicholson Screenwriting Award. He lives happily in a log cabin in the lake region of north New Jersey.